W9-CBI-554

What's the point?

Dinah was an environmentalist. In sixth grade she had helped start their school recycling program. But what was the point of recycling paper to save trees if all the trees were just going to be consumed anyway in an all-consuming fire?

Dinah was an actress. She loved to be in plays. Someday she would be in movies. But what was the point of making a movie if there was no one left on earth to see it?

Birth-Dawn-Spring. Dinah would have to write a new poem: Death-Night-Winter. But what was the point of poetry if there would be no one left on the charred, lifeless earth to read it?

Footprints in the sands of time. Why should Dinah care if she left any, if in another five billion years-only five!-no one would know or care whether she had left any or not?

Dinah Forever

Dinah Forever

Claudia Mills

SCHOLASTIC INC.

New York Toronto London Auckland Sydney
Mexico City New Delhi Hong Kong

No part of this publication may be reproduced in whole or in part, or stored in a retrieval system, or transmitted in any form or by any means, electronic, mechanical, photocopying, recording, or otherwise, without written permission of the publisher. For information regarding permission, write to Hyperion Books for Children, an imprint of Buena Vista Books, Inc., 114 Fifth Avenue, New York, NY 10011.

ISBN 0-439-21792-X

Copyright © 1995 by Claudia Mills.
All rights reserved.
Published by Scholastic Inc., 555 Broadway, New York, NY 10012,
by arrangement with Hyperion Books for Children,
an imprint of Buena Vista Books, Inc.
SCHOLASTIC and associated logos are trademarks
and/or registered trademarks of Scholastic Inc.

12 11 10 9 8 7 6 5 4 3 2 1   0 1 2 3 4 5/0

Printed in the U.S.A.   40

First Scholastic printing, April 2000

The text for this book is set in Perpetua.

For all my friends
in the Class of 1972,
North Plainfield High School,
North Plainfield, New Jersey

Dinah Forever

One

Dinah planned to save Nick Tribble's postcards forever. She would keep them under her pillow every night and read them over every day, for the rest of her life. Then, if she ever died, she would have the postcards buried with her in her grave. They could be neatly thumbtacked to the inside of the coffin, message side out, or maybe placed on her chest, just over her heart.

There were two postcards, only two, from the whole entire summer, but Nick had told her before he left that he wasn't good at writing. Lying on Mrs. Briscoe's lumpy couch, flat on her back, as if posing for her coffin, Dinah read both cards over again for the hundred-thousandth time.

The first card had come from London, England. On the front was a picture of the Changing of the Guard at Buckingham Palace. On the back, Nick had written:

Dear Ocean-River,

   I tried to get one of these guys to crack up, but I couldn't do it.

                              Nick

"Ocean-River" was supposed to be a joke, because Dinah's last name was Seabrooke.

The second card had come from Stonehenge, England. On the front was a picture of huge slabs of rock, standing in a circle, pointing upward toward the sky. On the back, Nick had written:

Dear Frizz Head,

   Don't let one of these fall on you.

                              Love,
                              Nick

Another joke, because Dinah's dark hair was curly. But "*Love*, Nick" didn't sound like a joke to Dinah at all.

They were Dinah's first postcards ever from a boy —and her first postcards ever from a boy who was supposed to be her boyfriend. But Dinah had hated Nick until almost the end of sixth grade, and then Nick had left with his family to spend the summer in England. So he hadn't really been her boyfriend for more than three weeks total. Now seventh grade was about to begin on Monday, only two days away, and Dinah would see Nick again, for the first time in almost three months.

Dinah looked at Mrs. Briscoe, sitting across the cozy,

4

cluttered room in her straight-backed chair next to the window. Mrs. Briscoe was thin and delicate-boned, with quick, bright eyes and a crest of snowy white hair; she reminded Dinah of a small, friendly bird. She had been one of Dinah's closest friends for almost a year, ever since she had become a client of Dinah's mother. Dinah's mother was an organization consultant, whose job was to help disorganized people get organized. Although Mrs. Briscoe was eighty-three years old, she didn't feel like an extra grandmother; she felt like a real friend, but even better in some ways, because she had lived so long and knew so much about life.

Dinah propped the postcards against the back of the couch, finding space for them amid Mrs. Briscoe's jumble of faded patchwork pillows. "Do you think—" Dinah stopped, and then tried again. "I haven't seen Nick in such a long time. He may have forgotten all about me."

Dinah hoped Mrs. Briscoe would laugh and say, "Forget *you*? How could he forget Dynamite Dinah?"

Mrs. Briscoe laughed. "Forget *you*, Dinah? You and I both know that's impossible."

Dinah was pleased, but not yet completely reassured. "Just because he remembers me doesn't mean he'll still *like* me."

Dinah waited for Mrs. Briscoe to laugh again and say, "To love Dinah once is to love her forever!" Or something like that.

But this time Mrs. Briscoe got up from her chair and came to perch on the edge of the sofa next to Dinah.

"I have a feeling Nick still likes you," Mrs. Briscoe said. "But as far as that goes, you may not like *him* anymore. Sometimes a spring romance fades over the summer."

Dinah felt mildly annoyed. What did the *season* of a romance have to do with anything?

"What season was it when you started dating Mr. Briscoe?" she asked. Mr. Briscoe had been dead for over ten years, but Dinah loved to hear stories about their long-ago courtship and marriage.

"Spring," Mrs. Briscoe admitted with a smile. "To this day I can't see a crab apple tree in bloom without thinking of Eddie, bringing me an enormous, messy bouquet of blossoms for my room."

"See?" Dinah asked. "And how long were you married?"

"Fifty-one years," Mrs. Briscoe said.

"See?" Dinah said again. She felt somehow that she had proved something about herself and Nick. Not that Nick had ever brought her flowers. But he *had* kissed her.

"Do you remember the first time Mr. Briscoe kissed you?" Dinah asked.

"Oh, my, yes," Mrs. Briscoe said. "But of course we were already engaged. Back then a fellow didn't kiss a girl unless he planned on marrying her."

"Oh," Dinah said. Well, things were different now. But even nowadays, she didn't think a boy would kiss a girl—seven times—unless he planned to keep on liking her for a long, long time. At least she hoped so.

6

Back at home that afternoon, Dinah was reading Nick's postcards over again when the telephone rang. Dinah snatched up the receiver on the second ring.

"Ocean-River! I'm back! It's me, Nick!"

As if anyone else called Dinah Ocean-River.

"Hi," Dinah said, trying to keep her voice calm and casual.

There was a pause on the other end of the line, and then Nick said, "So."

"So," Dinah echoed.

"So when we drove in from the airport last night, we passed that carnival thing down by City Hall. Do you want to go?"

"Sure."

"Like tonight? After supper? Like at seven o'clock?"

"Okay."

"See you then, Frizz Head."

It felt good to be correcting Nick again. "My hair isn't frizzy, it's—"

"Curly." Nick finished the sentence for her. "Bye."

"Bye," Dinah said.

Ha! Nick wouldn't have called her if he didn't like her. Or asked her to go to the carnival with him, just the two of them, like a date. Or called her Ocean-River and Frizz Head. This hardly sounded like a spring romance that had faded over the summer.

Dinah ran downstairs to tell her parents that Nick had called. Her mother sighed. Her father grinned. Her eighteen-month-old brother, Benjamin, looked at her solemnly, his thumb jammed in his chocolate-rimmed mouth.

Dinah called her best friend, Suzanne Kelly, and she and Suzanne analyzed the phone conversation syllable by syllable.

"He still likes you," Suzanne agreed. "I'd say he still likes you a *lot*."

Then, after a quick salad supper, Dinah took a cool shower and debated with herself what she should wear, even though she and Suzanne had spent ten minutes on the same question not an hour earlier. Finally Dinah put on the cutoff shorts and Ocean City T-shirt that Suzanne had recommended.

She studied herself in the mirror. She looked the same. Would Nick look the same? What would she say to him? What would he say to her? She tried to recall the kinds of things they had said to each other last spring. They had teased each other, and debated capital punishment together, and Nick had kissed her those seven times. They must have had regular conversations, too, but about what?

Dinah honestly couldn't remember. But she had probably told Nick many of her amazing and entertaining stories. Dinah was the kind of person who always had a story to tell. It wasn't bragging to say this, because it happened to be true. And Nick had probably laughed, the way Suzanne and Mrs. Briscoe and her parents always laughed. She could imagine him now, shaking his head with amused disbelief, saying, "You're something else, Ocean-River!"

Dinah thought back over her summer. She could tell Nick about the talent show she and Suzanne had put on at the nursing home. But that *was* a braggy story, because one of the old ladies there had called Dinah "the next Sarah Bernhardt," and afterward Dinah had found out that Sarah Bernhardt had once been the world's greatest actress. Maybe Dinah wouldn't tell Nick *that*. She didn't want him to think she was showing off.

But she definitely could tell him the story about how loud she had screamed in the haunted house at Ocean City. Or about the time she had baby-sat Benjamin for an hour, and he had emptied an entire box of crumbled saltine crackers all over her parents' bed. Or how she had walked across a river on a log during one of their family camping trips and had almost lost her balance and fallen in and drowned. It's true that the stream had been very shallow, but you can drown in a *bathtub* if you aren't careful.

The doorbell rang.

Dinah's heart stopped beating.

"Dinah!" her mother called. "Nick is here!"

Dinah started downstairs. Sure enough, there he was, her supposed real live boyfriend, standing in front of the window.

"Hi," Dinah said.

"Hi," Nick said.

Dinah stole a look at him. Same dark hair, same square glasses, same quick grin. He had grown taller over the summer. She met Nick's eyes. He was observing her just as she was observing him.

"Do you still want to walk over to the carnival?" Nick asked.

"Uh-huh," Dinah said, trying not to show how nervous she felt.

She called good-bye to her parents and Benjamin, and she and Nick headed out the door.

The Riverdale summer carnival was held in the parking lot next to City Hall, a quarter of a mile or so from Dinah's house. Dinah wondered if Nick would hold her hand as they walked there, but he didn't, and she was just as glad. It was too hot for holding hands. The Maryland sun, even in the evening, was sweltering as she and Nick hiked up the steep hill to the heart of town.

Dinah quickly reviewed her summer stories again. She would begin with "The Scream at the Haunted House." It even had a great title. But before Dinah could deliver the opening line, Nick broke the silence himself.

"I went punting on the river in Oxford," he told Dinah. "You know, where the big, famous university is? A punt is a kind of boat, sort of like a rowboat but flat-bottomed, and instead of oars you use this big, long pole that you stick down in the bottom of the river to push the boat along. Well, I dropped the pole by mistake, and it floated away out of my reach, so finally I had to jump out of the boat and swim to get it. A bunch of tourists stood on the banks and cheered."

10

Dinah couldn't help being impressed, but she felt jealous, too. She had never been to England. She had never been farther away from Maryland than Williamsburg, Virginia. And she had never been cheered by a crowd.

"That's really great. Well, Suzanne and I went to the haunted house at the boardwalk in Ocean City. The scariest part in it is when you walk through this long dark hallway at the end, and then all of a sudden this skeleton jumps out of a closet right in front of you. Well, the man who runs the haunted house said that in all his seventeen years in business, no one had ever screamed louder than I did when the skeleton jumped out. When Suzanne and I went back a week later, he said his ears were still ringing."

Dinah waited for Nick to ask for his own personal screaming demonstration.

Instead, Nick only said, "Wow! Oh, another really wild thing that happened: I rode on a double-decker bus all by myself in London, and the bus broke down by Piccadilly Circus, and it took me four hours to find my way back to our bed-and-breakfast and by then my parents had called the police."

Dinah wasn't even a little bit impressed this time. Anybody could get lost. Even Benjamin could get lost.

She plunged ahead without comment. "We put on a talent show for Mrs. Briscoe's friends at the nursing home—you know, the place she stayed last fall when she broke her leg. It was me, and Suzanne, and Greg, and Blaine, and a couple of other kids. I recited three really long poems."

Dinah hadn't meant to add the next line—in fact, she had meant *not* to add it—but she heard herself saying, "One old lady called me 'the next Sarah Bernhardt.'"

"Who's Sarah Bernhardt?" Nick asked.

Dinah tried to sound modest, but it was difficult. "The most famous actress who ever lived. The greatest actress in the history of the world."

They reached the carnival. It wasn't a very big one—just a small Ferris wheel and a couple of other rides, a row of booths where you could play games to win huge stuffed animals, and a row of booths that sold popcorn and ice cream and cotton candy and fresh-squeezed lemonade. Nick bought two ice-cold lemonades, and Dinah bought an enormous tub of hot buttered popcorn to share. They kept on walking and talking as they ate.

Halfway through Nick's *fourth* story about his adventures in England, Dinah had pretty much decided that this was one spring romance that couldn't fade fast enough to suit her. Dinah had the feeling that Nick had barely listened to her stories. Of course, she had barely listened to *his* stories. But other people's trips, frankly, weren't very interesting. Dinah's father still complained about the time her uncle had shown them three hours of slides from his cruise to Alaska.

Dinah and Nick bought tickets to play some of the games. They both hurled balls at a moving target and missed. They both swung a huge mallet on the Strength-o-Meter. Neither of them rang the bell, but Dinah scored Pretty Pathetic, while Nick scored Muscle Man.

Then they each got a slice of cream pie to throw in a clown's face. If you hit the clown through the small hole framing his face, you could win a stuffed bear bigger than Benjamin.

"You go first," Nick said, "pathetic one."

Dinah knew Nick was teasing, but she didn't find his remark even the slightest bit amusing.

"*You* go first," she said, "*braggy* one."

Nick stopped. "Wait a minute. I didn't say I was a muscle man. The Strength-o-Meter said I was a muscle man."

"I'm not talking about that," Dinah said. "I'm talking about everything else."

"Like what?"

"Like England, England, England, England, England. How you saved the Tower of London from burning. How you had a private audience with the queen."

"Let me get this straight," Nick said. "The next Sarah Somebody, the greatest actress in world history, thinks that *I'm* bragging?"

If Dinah hadn't had a slice of coconut cream pie, thick with whipped cream, right in her hand, the quarrel might have ended differently. She wouldn't have gone out of her way to hurl a slice of pie in Nick's smirking face. But she *did* have a piece of pie in her hand, and Nick's smirk was only five feet away.

Dinah hesitated only a moment. Then she let the pie fly. She didn't linger to see what Nick might decide to do with his piece of pie. She turned and ran. Nick didn't run after her.

Dinah didn't know whether she felt angrier with Nick or with herself, for ever having liked him. She did know that when she got home, she was going to tear Nick's two postcards into a million tiny pieces.

Two

Dinah's parents were sitting together in the family room when she arrived home from the carnival. It was pleasantly peaceful in the house, with Benjamin in bed.

"You're back early," her mother said. "You're all flushed. You haven't been running, have you? Not in this heat."

"Where is young Nicholas?" her father asked.

Her parents looked at each other, bewildered. Then Dinah saw comprehension dawn in their faces.

"Ah-ha," Dinah's father said. "A lovers' quarrel."

Dinah glared at him. "Nick and I are not *lovers*, and we didn't *quarrel*." It wasn't a quarrel, really, when you threw a piece of cream pie into someone's face. It was more like the first strike in a nuclear war.

"Don't tease her, Jerry." Dinah's mother moved over on the couch to make room for Dinah next to her. "Do you want to tell us about it?"

As a matter of fact, Dinah did. She had to admit that it was one of her better stories, right up there with all the wonderful summer stories that Nick hadn't even wanted to hear. But for some reason, she felt near tears when she was finished.

"Oh, Dinah," her mother said. "That doesn't sound like a very constructive way to resolve a disagreement."

"I didn't really mean to throw it," Dinah said. "It's almost like it threw itself."

"Maybe if you apologized to Nick," her father said. "Take him another piece of pie tomorrow. Kind of like a peace offering." He seemed pleased with this suggestion.

"I'm not apologizing to anyone," Dinah said. "If I gave Nick a piece of pie, he'd throw it in *my* face. It's just over, that's all."

Her father grinned.

"It *is*. Sometimes things *are*, you know." Dinah swallowed hard. Her own words sounded so bleak and final.

"Well, maybe it's for the best," her mother said. "You and Nick—in some ways you're so much alike, maybe too much alike. There were bound to be some stormy times, sooner or later."

Dinah thought this over. Were she and Nick too much *alike*? They hadn't seemed very much alike half an hour ago: Nick had only been interested in talking about Nick, while Dinah had been much more interested in talking about Dinah. Though maybe that *was* a way of being alike, after all.

In *Little Women*, Dinah suddenly remembered, Jo

refused to marry Laurie because she and Laurie were too much alike, both with strong wills and hot tempers. Dinah and Nick were alike in that way, too.

And their stormy times had definitely come sooner rather than later.

Upstairs in her room, Dinah took Nick's postcards out from under her pillow. It was time to rip them each into a million pieces. She'd do the Buckingham Palace card first; it was the one Nick had sent her first. Or maybe she'd do the Stonehenge card first. It was the one that had the word *love* on it. Dinah read both cards over again, trying to decide. Maybe she should just close her eyes and rip them both together.

But—in a way it was stupid to rip up somebody's postcards just because you hated him. It wasn't the postcards' fault that the boy who had written them had turned out to be so unworthy of her affections. Why take out her feelings on two helpless little rectangles of glossy cardboard?

Dinah reread the messages on the cards one last time. Then she buried the cards underneath a stack of sweaters in her bottom bureau drawer.

Sunday morning, early, while her parents and Benjamin were still asleep, Dinah got up and wrote them a note saying that she was walking over to Mrs. Briscoe's house. It was cooler than it had been the night before, and the dew was thick on the tangle of wildflowers in Mrs. Briscoe's small, unkempt front yard. Mrs. Briscoe was a morning person—up before dawn and in bed not much past dark—so Dinah knew it was all right to ring her bell at seven-thirty in the morning.

"Dinah, come in!" Mrs. Briscoe ushered Dinah into her untidy kitchen and began brewing a pot of tea.

Mrs. Briscoe drank hot tea summer and winter, and now Dinah did, too. Mrs. Briscoe never made tea with a tea bag. She made it the proper English way, with loose tea in a tea ball, steeped in a real china teapot. But Mrs. Briscoe's teapot wasn't a proper English teapot: It was in the shape of a cheerful, plump, bright green bullfrog. Mrs. Briscoe had a wonderful collection of all kinds of frogs and toads.

Dinah waited until she had a steaming teacup in front of her. "Nick and I had a fight," she began.

When she had told the story to her parents last night, her father had looked amused and her mother had looked worried. Mrs. Briscoe just listened. Maybe the best relationships came when one person was a talker and one was a listener. Dinah was a talker, obviously. Mrs. Briscoe was a listener. Suzanne was a listener. Nick was a talker. That alone explained a lot about their breakup.

"So you were right after all," Dinah finished. "It did fade over the summer."

"Maybe," Mrs. Briscoe said. "But sometimes it can take a while to get used to someone again, when you've been apart. I remember when Eddie came home from the war, I expected to be wild with joy about having him with me again, safe and sound. And then all we did was quarrel, about nothing at all, for months on end."

"You didn't throw a pie in his face, did you?" Dinah asked hopefully.

"No, but I did set his suitcase out on the front stoop one morning—we were living in Baltimore—and he had to go out in his pajamas to retrieve it. And then I bolted the front door behind him."

Dinah took the first sip of her now-lukewarm tea. It was funny to imagine gentle-voiced Mrs. Briscoe so fiery. "What happened then?"

"Then from my front window I saw my nosy neighbor, Lillian Sawhurst, coming out with her broom to sweep—and to spy. I felt so mortified that I opened the front door faster than it takes to tell it and let Eddie back in again."

"Was he mad?"

Mrs. Briscoe took the last sip of her own tea. "He was mad," she said, "but he and I both had quick, hot tempers, and those kinds of folks never stay mad for long."

So Mr. and Mrs. Briscoe had both had hot tempers. That worked against Dinah's theory.

"Would you say that Mr. Briscoe was a talker or a listener?"

"Oh, Eddie was a talker. He could talk harder and faster than anyone I ever met, until you, Dinah. That was the hardest thing for me to get used to after he died—the *silence* in the house. All day long, every day, the house was so *quiet*."

Mrs. Briscoe had tears in her eyes. Dinah looked away. She wanted to say something comforting, but Mrs. Briscoe was better at comforting her than she was at comforting Mrs. Briscoe.

"That's all right, Dinah," Mrs. Briscoe said. "I love talking about Eddie, even when the memories are sad ones. And my house has been a lot less quiet since I met you."

Back home again, in time for a second breakfast, Dinah called Suzanne, but she was already at church. Benjamin was in his high chair, pushing buttons at random on his toy tape recorder. Her father was sitting next to him, at the kitchen table, trying to read the first chapter of his brand-new biology book. After ten years in the Navy and another ten years of working as the manager of a sporting goods store, Dinah's father was going back to college to finish his undergraduate degree. He was still keeping the same schedule at the store, so he had to use every spare minute at home to study.

He looked up from his book as Dinah came into the kitchen. "I got your note. You were up and out early this morning," he said.

"I wanted to talk to Mrs. Briscoe." Dinah toasted herself an English muffin and sat down next to her father at the table.

"How's biology?" she asked.

"Do you know," her father said, "that I am the only male in my class not wearing a baseball cap backward?"

"You could do it," Dinah said. "You have a million baseball caps down at the store."

Her father shook his head. "Forty is the cutoff for backward baseball caps. I have to admit that I'm feeling rather ancient these days. And these young kids in my class are a lot more used to hitting the books than I am. But maybe age will turn out to have some advantages, as well. Let's see how I do on my first exam."

The morning dragged on. Dinah kept calling Suzanne's house, but Suzanne wasn't back from church yet. She called Blaine Yarborough, another friend from school, but Blaine wasn't home, either. Dinah's father finished the first chapter in his biology book and started on the second one. Her mother was making her usual thorough list of everything to do for the week ahead. Benjamin was involved in his own project, taking Duplos from the big Duplo tub, putting them all into an old shoe box, then taking them out of the shoe box and putting them back into the tub again.

Dinah wondered what Nick was doing. Had he torn up *her* two postcards—the one from Ocean City and the one from the Inner Harbor in Baltimore? Probably he had never even saved them in the first place.

"Can I take Benjamin out for a walk in the stroller?" Dinah asked.

Her mother glanced out the kitchen window at the thermometer. "It's awfully hot out."

"Just for a little walk."

Benjamin was already by the kitchen door, his

Duplo-transfer project abandoned. He loved his stroller.

Dinah's mother rubbed sun block on Benjamin's legs and arms, while Dinah dabbed his chubby cheeks. "Keep the awning up over him," her mother said.

Outside, the heat and humidity weighed on Dinah like a sopping wet blanket. She walked to Suzanne's house, one block down and one block over. No one answered the doorbell there. Then she found herself walking another block to Nick's street, Barclay Court. Maybe Nick would be outside, shooting baskets at the hoop hung over his garage, in a pathetic effort to overcome his grief at losing her.

He wasn't.

Maybe he was inside, ripping up postcards. Dinah wasn't about to ring his bell to find out. Afraid he might have seen her from a front window, she turned and hastily pushed Benjamin's stroller back to neutral territory.

Just as she had reached her own street, she saw him, walking down the hill toward her, his hands jammed in the pockets of his baggy shorts.

He saw her, too. Dinah met his eyes for one second. Then she looked away. Unless one of them crossed to the other side of the street, or stepped aside, or turned to flee, they would walk right smack into each other in two more minutes.

Dinah made herself keep on walking. Now she and Nick were on the same block. The sidewalk wasn't wide enough for her to pass him with the stroller. Would

Nick step aside or would she? Or would they collide head-on like two locomotives barreling toward each other on a single stretch of track?

Dinah looked up. Nick was standing still, right in front of her, blocking her way. She couldn't tell if he looked mad or not. He wasn't smiling, but he wasn't frowning, either. Dinah didn't think she could bear it if he walked past her without speaking.

"Frizz Head," Nick said, almost like a question.

Dinah knew then what she had to say next. "I—I'm sorry about—the pie." And suddenly she *was* sorry. You can't go around throwing pies at people whenever they don't act exactly the way you want them to act. She couldn't hate Nick for being a talker, when she was a talker, too. Maybe it was *good* to be alike, even if this sometimes made for a stormy relationship.

"Just remember, I owe you one," Nick said. "Sometime, someplace, there's a big fat piece of cream pie out there with your name on it."

"Oh, there is, is there?" Dinah asked, so happy that she felt like dancing in the ninety-five-degree midday heat, as Nick fell into step beside her, pushing the stroller home.

Three

Dinah had been so busy breaking up with Nick and then getting back together with him again that she was almost surprised to find herself standing at the bus stop Monday morning with Suzanne, waiting for the first day of seventh grade to begin. Seventh grade! Not that seventh grade was all that alarming. It wasn't like sixth grade, when everyone had to get used to the whole new world of a whole new school. Seventh grade was just—seventh grade, a comfortable in-between kind of year.

Even though Dinah and Suzanne each had a boy-friend this year—Nick for Dinah and Greg Thomas for Suzanne—they sat together on the bus as they had every year since they had become best friends back in third grade. But Dinah was conscious of Nick sitting a few rows behind her. It was strange and wonderful to think that there was a boy on this very bus who had kissed her just the night before.

"I'm still scared," Suzanne confessed to Dinah. "I don't care if we *are* seventh graders. We're still going to have new classes and new teachers. Tom told me that seventh-grade math is practically like algebra."

Suzanne's older brother Tom was a senior in high school.

"And it's, like, in seventh grade you have no *excuse* for anything anymore. In sixth grade you mess up and everyone says, 'Oh, she's just a sixth grader.' Now they'll say, 'Hey, you, how come you're still messing up in seventh grade?' "

"We won't mess up," Dinah said. "We'll make Tom help us with math if we need it. You'll be elected class secretary again, and Blaine'll be president, and we'll get all the best parts in Drama Club, and Nick and I are going to be the champions of the debate team. Mr. Roemer might as well clear out the front display case right now to make room for all our trophies."

Suzanne laughed. "It'll be better than sixth grade," she agreed.

Homerooms were assigned alphabetically; Suzanne wasn't in Dinah's homeroom, but Nick was. Their homeroom teacher this year was their social studies teacher from last year, Mr. Dixon, who also would be the coach for the new debate team. When Dinah heard the principal, Mr. Roemer, clear his throat over the PA system before saying, "Please rise and salute the flag," her heart sang with joy at the familiarity of it all.

Dinah had loved morning announcements ever since the first day of sixth grade. She listened with eager anticipation as Mr. Roemer read, "I want to call to your attention that our school has been *thoroughly* cleaned over the summer. *All* offensive remarks have been removed from lavatory doors. *All* gum has been removed from underneath classroom and library desks. Let me ask for your cooperation in maintaining these standards of cleanliness throughout the coming year, so that JFK Middle School will look as fresh and inviting in June as it does today."

Mr. Roemer's remarks gave Dinah a sudden keen longing for gum, with all its comic possibilities. Across the aisle from her, Nick pretended to take a wad of gum out of his mouth and stick it under his seat. Dinah's friend Blaine shook her head at him sternly. Nick pretended to pop the gum back into his mouth, with a wink at Dinah. It was just the kind of thing Dinah herself would have done. She smiled to herself.

Mr. Roemer read more: announcements about other rules, about the first soccer match of the season, about next week's activities fair. Then he said, "Let me end this morning's announcements by sharing with you a poem by the great American poet Henry Wadsworth Longfellow."

Dinah and Nick looked at each other. This was something new. Dinah couldn't remember any occasion in the past on which a poem had been part of morning announcements.

"The poem is called 'A Psalm of Life,' " Mr. Roemer said, making his voice sound extra grand and solemn.

"Tell me not, in mournful numbers,
Life is but an empty dream!
For the soul is dead that slumbers,
And things are not what they seem."

It was a long poem, and when Mr. Roemer finished, some of the boys sitting near Dinah made groaning, gagging noises. But Dinah sat enthralled. She hadn't understood all of the poem, but certain lines sang themselves over again in her head.

Lives of great men all remind us
We can make our lives sublime,
And, departing, leave behind us
Footprints on the sands of time.

Footprints on the sands of time! How could Henry Wadsworth Longfellow have known that that was precisely what Dinah planned to leave behind her during seventh grade?

It turned out that Dinah and Nick had three classes together—English, science, and math—as well as lunch. When Suzanne and Dinah ran to compare schedules after homeroom, they found that they had those same classes together, plus social studies. They hugged each other with relief.

Math, first period, looked hard, but Ms. Lewis was young and funny. She liked to talk with an exaggerated New York accent; she called the class "youse guys."

Ms. Dunne, the second-period English teacher,

looked young, too. Her bright red lipstick matched her bright red earrings, bright red blazer, and bright red shoes. When Dinah closed her eyes a moment to rest from all the bright red, she saw a ghostly negative of Ms. Dunne, a dark blob surrounded by a bright aura.

"I'm so glad that Mr. Roemer began our school year with a poem this morning," Ms. Dunne said. "We're going to be writing a great deal of poetry in seventh-grade English. To get us started, let's all take out a piece of paper and a writing utensil. Write a poem on any subject. I'm not going to be grading it. In fact, I never grade student poetry. Poetry isn't something you write for a grade. It's something you write for your soul."

Sitting in front of Dinah, Artie Adams snickered. Artie's soul had no poetry in it whatsoever.

Dinah had a very poetic soul—at least she thought she did—but she wasn't sure she could write a poem on command, at nine-thirty on a Monday morning. She used to try writing poems when she was younger, but she had always gotten stuck after the first line. Today she was stuck *before* the first line.

Glancing around the room, Dinah saw blank sheets of paper on every desk, even Blaine's. No one had written anything.

Nick put up his hand. Dinah felt proud of him for being the one to break the silence. "Don't we have to be—you know—*inspired* or something?"

Ms. Dunne shook her head. "Someone once said that

genius is ten percent inspiration and ninety percent perspiration. The same is true of poetry."

Nick's friend Jason Winfield sniffed loudly at his armpit. Ms. Dunne ignored him.

"Today I'm going to let you all flounder for a bit, to see how you make out by yourselves. But on other days I'll have a number of exercises to share with you, exercises to help get the poetic juices flowing. We'll be reading a lot of poetry, too, and that will help as well. I have taught seventh-grade English for ten years now, and one thing I have discovered is that there is a poet inside of *everybody*."

Artie thrust up his hand. Ms. Dunne consulted her seating chart. "Artie?"

"There is no poet inside of *me*," Artie said loudly.

Ms. Dunne smiled. "Every year some student tells me that on the first day of class, and every year that very student turns out to have a gift for poetry that he never even dreamed of."

That silenced Artie. Dinah stared at her empty sheet of paper.

"Do our poems have to rhyme?" someone else asked.

"How long do they have to be?"

"Can you give us kind of a suggestion for what they should be about?"

"A poem does not have to rhyme. It can be any length. As for a subject, how about *beginnings*? Now, that's all I'm going to say to you today. You have the rest of the period to write."

Beginnings. That helped a little. And it wasn't going to be graded.

Dinah picked up her pen and scribbled one word, then another. Five minutes later she was done. She read her poem over to herself.

Beginnings

Birth—
Dawn—
Spring—
Deep in my heart
A tiny voice
Begins to sing.
For this is
The start of
Everything.

It wasn't as good as "footprints on the sands of time," but it was pretty good for a first try, on the first day of seventh grade. It was a good *beginning*.

Dinah had Miss Brady again, from sixth grade, for gym during third period, and her same teacher from last year, Mr. Maurer, for fourth-period music. Even the food at lunch was the same as the food from sixth grade. The lukewarm macaroni-and-beef casserole and stale cherry pie could have been left over from the last day of school in June. But last year, Dinah and her friends had eaten at an all-girls table. This year, Greg

Thomas came over to sit with Suzanne, and Nick took the empty seat next to Dinah. Nick picked up his plate of pie and weighed it thoughtfully in his hand, as if deciding whether to eat it or to throw it. Dinah felt herself blushing.

After lunch, Dinah had study hall and then social studies, with a different teacher from last year, a dignified older man named Mr. McGowan, who wore a small, neat, polka-dot bow tie.

The last period of the day, eighth period, was science. Dinah's science teacher, Mr. Mubashir, was a small, slim man with smooth, dark skin and a slight foreign twist to his speech. He spoke quickly, too, so Dinah had to listen carefully to understand what he was saying.

Mr. Mubashir was as enthusiastic about science as Ms. Dunne was about poetry. In seventh-grade science they were going to study astronomy for the first half of the year and earth science for the second half. Mr. Mubashir promised that seventh-grade science students would learn many astonishing and amazing things.

"How many of you think that the earth revolves around the sun?" Mr. Mubashir asked the class.

Everyone put up a hand.

"How many of you could *prove* it to someone who insisted that the sun revolved around the earth?"

No one put up a hand. Mr. Mubashir looked pleased.

"How many of you know why we have seasons here on earth?"

Dinah thought a moment. Because the earth revolves

around the sun? Because the earth is round? Because it would be too boring not to have seasons and to have life always be the same?

The class fidgeted. Dinah wished that Mr. Mubashir would just tell them the answer.

Then the quietest boy that Dinah had ever met, Todd Burstyn, gave the smallest possible signal with his hand. "Because the earth tilts on its axis," he said in a low voice.

Mr. Mubashir chuckled with satisfaction. "Quite right! Quite right! And we will explain it to all of you this fall so that you, too, will know why we have seasons on earth, and why we will continue to have them for a good while yet." Mr. Mubashir paused for effect. "But not forever, my friends. Not forever. And why is that?"

Dinah found herself getting interested in the question, even though she didn't generally think of herself as a science person. Maybe the answer had to do with global warming. Dinah had gotten involved with environmental issues back in sixth grade, and she knew that people were actually causing the climate to change by making so much air pollution.

She raised her hand. "Because of global warming?"

"Ahh," Mr. Mubashir said. "The effects of our human actions on our climate—a fascinating question. We will explore it together next spring. Yes, you might say that our seasons will end because of global warming. But this warming will not be caused by anything we humans do. The ultimate energy crisis is coming, my friends. Our sun is a star, like all other stars, and no star can live forever. Someday—not too soon!—but in another five billion years, our sun is going to run out of hydrogen. This will cause chemical changes that will make our sun swell up into a red giant a hundred times its present size. Here on earth, the continents will melt, the oceans will boil away, the entire planet will be vaporized. Then our sun will contract into a white dwarf, give up the last of its heat, and die."

Dinah's hand was in the air again. "But what will *we* do? What will happen to *us*?"

"We will not be here. No life will be here. Life on earth will no longer be possible. But we will learn more about these things this fall. And we will have trips, yes? We will visit the National Air and Space Museum. And we will go out together in the nighttime to see the stars."

Mr. Mubashir began passing out the science textbooks. Dinah took hers automatically. Mr. Mubashir kept on talking, but Dinah couldn't listen. She felt cold inside, cold beyond shivering, as if the dying sun had already surrendered the last of its heat into the vastness of space.

Dinah was an environmentalist. In sixth grade she had helped start their school recycling program. But what was the point of recycling paper to save trees if all the trees were just going to be consumed anyway in an all-consuming fire?

Dinah was an actress. She loved to be in plays. Someday she would be in movies. But what was the point of making a movie if there would be no one left on earth to see it?

Birth—Dawn—Spring. Dinah would have to write a new poem: Death—Night—Winter. But what was the point of poetry if there would be no one left on the charred, lifeless earth to read it?

Footprints on the sands of time. Why should Dinah care if she left any, if in another five billion years—only five!—no one would know or care whether she had left any or not?

Four

After the final bell, Dinah walked numbly to her locker. She loaded her new textbooks into her backpack, hardly seeing the crowds of students who raced past her.

Suzanne seemed perfectly normal as she led the way to the bus. "Well, we survived the first day," Suzanne said cheerfully. "Ms. Lewis is nice! Math isn't going to be so bad. I didn't get one single mean teacher. Isn't Mr. Mubashir sweet? My poem in English class was just four lines long, though. But Ms. Dunne said they could be any length."

Dinah didn't say anything. So they had survived *one day*. If Mr. Mubashir was right, one day down meant one day closer to the end—of everything.

"Did you notice how *little* the sixth graders looked? And they *run* everywhere. I helped one of them find her homeroom this morning, and she was almost *crying*."

Dinah kept on walking.

"Dinah!" Suzanne shook her arm. "What's wrong? It's not—you and Nick didn't have another fight, did you?"

Dinah shook her head. They boarded the bus and took seats together halfway back. Nick got on the bus after them. He touched Dinah's shoulder lightly as he walked toward a seat in the rear.

Dinah finally found her voice. "What Mr. Mubashir said, in science class—do you think it's true?"

"What did he say?" Suzanne asked. "He just gave us the books and explained about how he grades. Oh, that stuff at the beginning? I'm sure it's true. Tom said that Mr. Mubashir is the smartest teacher in the school. He knows everything there is to know about science."

How could Suzanne sound so unconcerned if she had heard the same news Dinah had heard? Dinah tried one more time. "So you really think the *sun* is going to *die*?"

"Well, I guess it has to," Suzanne said. "Like Mr. Mubashir said, it has to run out of fuel someday. But it's not going to happen for a long time. I bet life on earth will end way before that. A comet will hit the earth, or we'll blow ourselves up with a nuclear bomb, or something."

This was Suzanne's idea of a *comforting* remark?

"*Dinah*," Suzanne said. "You can't worry about something that's going to happen five *billion* years from now. And, anyway, it's not like we can do anything about it. Do you want to cover books at your house or mine?"

"It doesn't matter," Dinah said.

Nothing did.

They went to Suzanne's house. The snacks were always better at Suzanne's house. After three large, soft homemade oatmeal raisin cookies washed down with a tall glass of milk, Dinah felt slightly better. Suzanne's brother Tom sat down with them in the kitchen to listen to their first-day-of-school stories. Tom was one of Dinah's biggest fans, almost as appreciative as Mrs. Briscoe. Today he understood Dinah's feelings better than Suzanne did.

"A solar system that's had Dynamite Dinah in it isn't just going to *end*," Tom said. "It'll find some way to keep on going."

"Like how?" Dinah asked.

"They'll think of something," Tom said. "Five billion years from now, people are going to have some awesome technology."

"Maybe they can send a bunch of rocket ships to get some hydrogen from some other solar system," Dinah said. Her mother always liked it when Dinah tried to come up with constructive ways to solve her problems. Perhaps she should forget about being an actress and think about being a rocket scientist instead.

"That sounds good," Tom said. "They'll pump it in on the Dinah Seabrooke Memorial Transgalactic Pipeline."

Dinah felt better enough then to eat two more cookies. She glanced out the window. The sun was still shining brightly. So far, so good.

Dinah's parents weren't worried about the end of the solar system.

"I just wish it would end before my first biology exam," her father said. "How anyone remembers the difference between meiosis and mitosis is beyond me."

Dinah's mother said, "Well, everything ends sometime. This gives us one more reason to use our time wisely now." She didn't seem to see that that was the whole problem. Why do *anything* if *everything* was going to come to *nothing*?

Nick came over after supper, just for half an hour, since it was a school night. Dinah waited to see if he would bring up the subject himself. He had been sitting right next to her as Mr. Mubashir had spoken. It was almost like a test. If Nick had the same reaction as Dinah to Mr. Mubashir's announcement, it would mean that they were alike in the right kind of way. If he didn't mind about the end of all life in the solar system, it would mean that they weren't alike enough, and their romance was destined to burn out as surely as the sun, only a lot sooner.

They sat together on Dinah's front porch, side by side on the porch swing. Dinah beamed her thoughts toward Nick, willing him to pass the test, to say the right thing.

"We have some pretty wild teachers this year," Nick said. "Did you see Artie's face when Dunne told him about his gift for poetry? And Mubashir—he's something else. If you tell your class on the first day that the whole solar system is going to end, what do you tell them on the second day?"

"I guess he could tell us that the whole universe is going to end." Dinah tried to keep her voice steady. Nick had noticed Mr. Mubashir's announcement, and he had mentioned it all by himself, without Dinah's prompting. That earned him, say, fifty points out of a hundred on Dinah's quiz. But now what would Nick say? Would he go on to tell Dinah that the news had left him shaken to the core of his being?

"How was your social studies guy?" Nick asked then. "I got Dixon again. He sure got himself all revved up over the summer."

So Nick was *not* shaken to the core of his being. He had passed the test—but just barely, without a point to spare. Dinah gave him a D minus.

Dinah couldn't let the subject drop, just like that. "Doesn't it make you feel strange at all to know that life on earth is going to *end*?"

"Sure," Nick said. "But maybe it *won't* end. Maybe we'll all pick up and move to some other solar system, one with a really young, energetic sun. That could be cool. When I moved to Maryland last year from California, it turned out to be cool. You meet crazy people when you move. Sometimes you like some of them."

Nick reached over and took Dinah's hand. Dinah felt suddenly shy. She decided to take back Nick's D-minus grade. He deserved at least a C minus, maybe even a C plus. If everyone on earth did move to another solar system, maybe the end of this one wouldn't be so terrible. Still, *Dinah* wouldn't be one of the ones moving to the cool new solar system. Neither would Nick, or Suzanne, or Tom, or Dinah's parents, or Benjamin, or Mrs. Briscoe.

Suddenly Dinah had a new and even more wrenching thought. The sun was going to die in five billion years, but she, Dinah Seabrooke, was in all likelihood going to die a lot sooner than that. So whatever happened to the sun, *she* wasn't going to be around to see it or to fix it or to mind it.

The second realization seemed as stunning and unbelievable as the first. At one level, Dinah had always taken for granted that she would die. But it had never seemed real to her that someday there would be no more *Dinah*. Now, somehow, for the first time, it did. The sun would burn out. And Dinah would burn out. *Everybody* died.

Dinah let Nick talk some more about the first day of school; then she managed to say good-bye. One day she, Dinah Marie Seabrooke, also known as Dynamite Dinah, was going to *die*. No transgalactic pipeline or relocation to another solar system could alter that one basic and irrevocable fact.

Dinah didn't have a chance to tell Mrs. Briscoe about the end of the solar system until after school on Friday. By then she was used to Ms. Lewis's tough-guy talk, Ms. Dunne's passion for poetry, and Mr. Mubashir's ability to come up daily with some astonishing new science fact. She felt as if she had been in seventh grade forever.

It was interesting having Ms. Dunne in the morning and Mr. Mubashir in the afternoon. Mr. Mubashir's science facts could practically be turned into poetry if you laid them out in a poetic way on the page. Dinah tried with one:

> The universe began
> As a teeny tiny pinprick
> Smaller than the nucleus
> Of a single atom
> And now it has a hundred billion galaxies
> Each containing a hundred billion stars.

At Mrs. Briscoe's house on Friday, Dinah curled up on the couch and tucked Mrs. Briscoe's crocheted afghan around her. It had turned chilly that afternoon, and the soft yarn of the afghan felt comforting around Dinah's bare knees.

"Do you want to hear some poems?" Dinah asked Mrs. Briscoe.

Mrs. Briscoe set the frog teapot next to a heap of old magazines on her small coffee table and poured out two cups of tea. "I certainly do," Mrs. Briscoe said, "especially if they're poems by you."

So Dinah read "Beginnings" and another new poem she was working on:

"In a mere five billion years,
The sun will burn out, like a light.
In a mere five billion years,
Our earth will lie in endless night.

My friends don't seem to understand
Why this makes me want to cry.
But isn't it a tragedy
That everything on earth will die?"

Dinah waited for Mrs. Briscoe's reaction. This time it wasn't a test. She really wanted to hear what Mrs. Briscoe would say. Mrs. Briscoe's own husband had died. If anyone would know about death, it was Mrs. Briscoe.

Mrs. Briscoe took a long time before answering. "I'm not sure what I think about death," she finally said. "Sometimes I feel like you do, that nothing should die, that everything should live forever."

"Well, maybe not everything," Dinah said. She didn't feel like drinking her tea yet, but she held her hands around her cup for the warmth. "I don't mind if ants die, or mosquitoes. But the *sun* should go on forever. And I want to go on forever. I mean, I kind of always expected to. Or maybe not *expected* to. But I didn't expect *not* to."

Mrs. Briscoe let Dinah's words settle in the air. Then she said, "Other times I feel that everything *should* die. We need to have beginnings; maybe we need to have endings, too."

Dinah must have looked dubious, because Mrs. Briscoe went on. "But lately I've been thinking that nothing really *does* die, that somehow, in some form, we all live on."

"Like in heaven?" Dinah asked. Dinah's family didn't go to church, the way Suzanne's did. Dinah didn't think her parents believed in God or heaven. But if there was a heaven, then it wouldn't be so bad leaving earth; it would be more like moving to a new and different solar system, the way Nick had suggested. Even so, Dinah still wanted earth to be there, the way it always had.

"There might be a heaven," Mrs. Briscoe said, "or maybe we just live on in the memories and lives of those who love us."

"But if the sun burns out, there won't *be* any more memories. There won't be any people to *have* memories."

"I see what you mean," Mrs. Briscoe said.

Dinah didn't know if she should ask her next question or not. "Do you think—Mr. Briscoe—do you think he's up in heaven?"

"I don't know," Mrs. Briscoe said, and Dinah could tell that it had been all right that she had asked. "I hope so. I know I don't feel that Eddie is really gone. But maybe it's because he's still in me, in my memories."

"It's hard, not *knowing*," Dinah said.

"I know," Mrs. Briscoe said softly. "I know. But I guess I'll find out myself before too long."

Dinah stared at her, appalled. "What do you mean?" she asked.

"I'm eighty-three," Mrs. Briscoe said in a calm, matter-of-fact voice. "Eddie died when he was seventy-four."

"But—" Dinah didn't know what to say. "Lots of people live until they're ninety. Or a hundred. Or those people in Russia who eat all the yogurt—they live until they're a hundred and ten."

"I don't want to live until I'm a hundred and ten," Mrs. Briscoe said.

"*I* want you to," Dinah said. Her voice came out choked with tears. The sun wasn't going to die for a long time, and neither was Dinah, but Mrs. Briscoe was old. However you counted it, eighty-three was old. How could Mrs. Briscoe not want to live until she was a hundred and ten? Dinah wanted to live until she was a *billion* and ten.

Mrs. Briscoe patted Dinah's hand with her veiny gnarled fingers.

"I don't want you to die for a long, long time," Dinah said. "I don't want you to *ever* die."

She turned and hugged Mrs. Briscoe as tightly as she could. Mrs. Briscoe hugged her back. For a long moment, neither of them spoke, and then Mrs. Briscoe gently pulled herself away.

Five

Wednesday morning, during the second week of school, the PA system clicked on in Dinah's homeroom, and Mr. Roemer cleared his throat. In sixth grade, all the students had learned to join him in a daily symphony of exaggerated phlegmy sounds. But by this year the joke had begun to wear thin. Dinah hoped that the new sixth graders in their homerooms were beginning the same tradition.

"Petitions for class office are due here on my desk at the close of eighth period a week from today," Mr. Roemer read. "There are four class officers: president, vice president, secretary, and treasurer. . . ."

A year ago, that same announcement had thrown Dinah into a frenzy of campaigning. The most important thing in her life had been her race for sixth-grade class president. She had planned on being the first girl president of her class, and she had promised to start the first schoolwide recycling program, and when she had been done with her glorious term of office, they were going to rename JFK Middle School in her honor.

Dinah smiled to herself sadly. In the end, Blaine Yarborough had won the election, not Dinah, and Blaine had been the first girl president, and Blaine had launched the recycling program. (Though JFK Middle School still bore its same name.) But Blaine had been a good president, probably far better than Dinah would have been. Blaine was so serious and sensible. Everyone respected Blaine. Someday Blaine would be president of the United States. Dinah had no doubt about it.

When Mr. Roemer finished talking, Dinah turned around to Blaine. "I want to be the first to sign your petition," she said.

Blaine shook her head. "I'm not running."

Dinah stared at her. "You're crazy. You'd win by a landslide."

"I don't think the same people should have offices all the time," Blaine said. "Especially president. Remember my platform last year? On school spirit? I really think *everyone* should be involved in running things. There shouldn't be one little clique that runs the whole school."

As usual, it was hard to disagree with Blaine. Blaine's conclusions always sounded like no more or less than the simple truth.

"But if one person is *best* at being president—" Dinah had an alarming thought. "And the recycling program. What if someone wins who doesn't care about recycling?" Last year, for a while, it had looked as if Jason Winfield would win the election, and Jason had even said out loud that he thought recycling was dumb.

"The program's already *there*," Blaine said. "It's a fact now. It can't *vanish*."

The bell rang. Dinah followed Blaine out to the hallway. "But recycling is just the *beginning*. There are a million other projects we could start. Like a campaign against using plastic utensils in the cafeteria. Or for planting more trees on the school grounds. Or—how about starting a JFK compost pile for all the food waste from everybody's cafeteria trays?"

"Do it," Blaine said seriously. "*You* be class president. It's your turn now. I'll campaign for you."

The idea was electrifying. Dinah felt a thrilling jolt of excitement at the very thought of it. She loved everything about campaigning: posters, buttons, attention-getting displays in the hall. And this year she would win, with Blaine behind her. She felt young again, full of hope again.

Did she have time to dash to the office to pick up a petition before first-period math? No. But if she hurried, she could do it between math and English.

For seventh-grade president: Dinah Seabrooke! Her campaign slogan: Save the planet!

Then Dinah remembered. Save the planet. Right. Save a few trees now so that more trees could burn in the sun's blazing inferno later.

Dinah didn't pick up a petition that morning, but she thought about it every time she walked past the main office. Suzanne didn't pick one up, either, although she had been a popular class secretary in sixth grade and probably could have won reelection.

"Blaine's right," Suzanne said promptly, when Dinah shared Blaine's news with her on the way to English class. "The same people *shouldn't* run everything all the time. But you should run, Dinah. You really should. I bet Nick thinks so, too."

Dinah thought about that for a minute. This year, if she ran, she would have Blaine behind her *and* Nick beside her. The boys wouldn't tease her as much if she had a boyfriend by her side, helping out in her campaign.

At lunch, Dinah swallowed her chicken nuggets and french fries. Then she turned to Nick. "Suzanne and Blaine think I should run for class president," she blurted out. "I don't think I'm going to, but I was just wondering what you think."

Nick grinned. "You'd be great," he said. "And if you were president, I could be First Gentleman. Waving from Air Force One! Fancy teas with the other First Gentlemen! A designer tux for the Inaugural Ball! Count me in! But—would I have to kiss babies? I'm not so good at kissing babies."

"You could practice on Benjamin," Dinah said, pleased at Nick's response. "He doesn't drool anywhere near as much as he used to."

Nick made a face. Then, his voice turning serious, he asked, "You don't want to run?"

Dinah shook her head slowly. "No. I did last year,

but it was different then. This year—it's like, if I ran, my platform would be environmental issues. You know, ways we could add to the recycling program. But there's no point to it anymore."

"What do you mean?" Nick asked. "Of course there's a point to it. Why wouldn't there be a point to it?"

"If the sun's just going to burn out *anyway* . . ."

"The *sun*?"

The bell rang. Nick and Dinah carried their trays to the conveyor belt. "Come on, Dinah," Nick said. "You can't let that stuff about the end of the solar system spoil my one and only chance of being First Gentleman."

Dinah had to laugh. But of course the real question wasn't who would be First Gentleman. The real question was who would be seventh-grade class president. Would it be Dinah?

The first Drama Club meeting of the year was held after school on Thursday. Last year both Suzanne and Dinah had had starring roles in the spring one-act play. But the fall play was always a musical, and that meant Dinah wouldn't get a part, even though she was the best actress in the seventh grade, maybe in the whole school. Dinah couldn't sing.

Dinah didn't want to go to the Thursday meeting, but Suzanne talked her into it.

"Maybe this time it won't be a musical," Suzanne said loyally. Suzanne didn't need to worry either way.

She was musical through and through. Her mother was a church organist and choir director. Suzanne herself was a wonderful pianist. And Suzanne had a clear, sweet soprano that never faltered.

Sure enough, after calling the meeting to order, Mrs. Bevens, the drama coach, announced that the fall play would be *Carousel*, a musical by Rodgers and Hammerstein. Dinah hardly listened as Mrs. Bevens told them the story of *Carousel*. But she had to admit that it was a pretty strange story, because one of the main characters dies partway through the play, yet he's still in it, watching over his wife and daughter, invisible to them but not to the audience. He can still sing up a storm, even though he's dead.

Mrs. Bevens played them some of the songs from *Carousel* on the tinny old upright piano that stood at the back of the drama room, singing the words in her quavery old-lady's voice. Dinah slumped down behind her desk. It wasn't terribly interesting hearing songs that other people would be singing.

But then Mrs. Bevens began singing a song so beautiful that sudden tears stung Dinah's eyes as she listened. The song was called "If I Loved You."

The idea behind the song was that the person singing it won't admit that she loves the person she's singing it to. She keeps talking about what she'd do *if* she loved him, making it sound as if she *doesn't*. But she sings about what she would do so movingly that anyone listening must know that she loves him very much already. The soaring melody matched the words perfectly.

It was Dinah's own song, Dinah and Nick's, because last year it had taken her weeks and weeks of telling everybody how much she hated Nick before she could tell herself that maybe she didn't hate him *quite* as much as she had announced to the world.

Auditions were to be held next week, reading auditions on Monday and singing auditions on Tuesday.

"Dinah," Suzanne whispered to her, "you don't mind if I try out, do you?" It was a delicate point, since only Suzanne could have a major, singing part.

Dinah shook her head. She felt a strange, hopeful stirring inside her. It was true that she had never been able to sing before, but she had never had a song like "If I Loved You" to sing. Maybe she had learned how to sing over the summer, without realizing it. If there was a poet inside of everyone, maybe there was also a singer inside of everyone.

"I might try out, too," Dinah told Suzanne. Suzanne looked surprised, but she didn't say anything.

Dinah tried singing "If I Loved You" to herself in her head. In her head, it sounded just fine.

Over the weekend, Dinah thought more about the election. So far, two kids had entered petitions to run for class president: Jason Winfield and some girl named Eliza Evans. Dinah knew Jason's views on recycling all too well; she didn't know anything about Eliza.

Should she run? Part of her wanted to run, with a dull ache of longing, but another part felt that she *couldn't* run, given the impending extinguishment of the solar system, not to mention the impending extinguishment of Dinah herself. The end of the solar system wasn't the kind of thing you could agonize about one week and then dismiss the next. "Oh, the sun burning out. Yeah, I was kind of worried about that for a couple of days."

Nick and Dinah went for a long walk together on Saturday evening, down to the big park by the public library. The days were getting shorter. By seven-thirty the first fireflies were beginning to blink in the falling darkness. Dinah and Nick both caught one and watched them glow inside their cupped hands for a few moments before letting them go. Then they sat on a park bench near the playground. Nick kissed Dinah. Kiss number nine? Or ten? Dinah was losing count. The kiss lasted a long time. That was one good thing about seventh grade. Seventh-grade kisses were longer than sixth-grade ones.

"So," Nick said then. "About the election. Do you think you'll run, or not?"

"Probably not," Dinah said. She tried to make her voice sound appropriately somber and gloomy, the voice of one who was renouncing all earthly ambition in the face of the impending cosmic tragedy. "It's like, what would I put on my posters? I can't tell people that I'll keep the sun from burning out. So why vote for me? *I* wouldn't even vote for me."

"It's not going to burn out for a long time," Nick reminded Dinah. "We can't just give up on everything else and wait for it all to end. I mean, people have always known they were going to die, but they still did great things with their lives."

"Yes, but . . ." Dinah let her sentence trail off. She didn't see how people *could* go on living their ordinary, everyday lives when death awaited everyone inescapably at the end.

"If you . . ." This time Nick was the one who let his sentence trail off. It was too dark now for Dinah to see the expression on his face. "If you *don't* run, I was thinking—I think you *should* run, but if you don't—well, I might give it a try."

Dinah was caught off guard. She had expected Nick to urge her one more time to put aside her private despair to assume the noble burden of public service. She hadn't expected Nick to be getting ready to assume that noble burden himself. If she wasn't president, obviously someone else would be—but Nick? If Nick was president, Dinah would be . . . First Lady. She didn't think she could stand it.

"You'd be great," Dinah said, forcing enthusiasm into her voice. What else could she do? Unless she could quickly perk up and announce cheerily that she didn't mind *so* much about the death of the solar system, after all. But she *did* mind. When she thought about the death of the sun, and her own death, and Mrs. Briscoe's, and the death of everyone else in the world, it was *shallow* to let herself care about anything else.

"Look," Nick said. "Petitions aren't due till Wednesday. I'll get one tomorrow, but I won't turn it in until you decide what you're going to do. Okay?"

"I've already decided," Dinah said in a flat voice.

Dinah had wanted to be president; now Nick would be president. Only one person could be president, and this year it would be Nick. If nothing mattered, anyway, as she kept insisting, why should Dinah suddenly feel so jealous of Nick, and when he was being so decent and reasonable, too?

"You might re-decide," Nick said. "I won't turn my petition in until three-eighteen on Wednesday."

So Dinah still had time to change her mind.

Six

The reading tryouts for *Carousel* were held after school on Monday. Dinah read for all the major girls' roles: Julie, Carrie, Nettie, Louise. Suzanne did, too. In Dinah's opinion, they both read better than any other seventh graders, and even better than any of the eighth graders. And of course the sixth graders had no chance whatsoever.

Nick didn't try out—very few boys did—so if Dinah somehow won the part of Julie, the one who sang "If I Loved You," she wouldn't get to sing it to Nick, as Billy, Julie's husband in the play. But in her heart she knew she would be singing it to Nick, whichever other boy actually played the role—even if Nick ended up running for class president in her place.

"You'll be Julie," Dinah told Suzanne on the bus ride home.

She waited for Suzanne to insist politely, "No, *you'll* be Julie." She and Suzanne had competed before for parts, so Dinah knew the etiquette of each pretending that she thought the other would get the part both wanted.

Suzanne looked uncomfortable. "You read the best today," Suzanne said.

Dinah knew that Suzanne was thinking about the voice auditions tomorrow. Reading was only half the audition this time. But surely sometimes a person who can't sing suddenly *finds* her voice. Dinah was positive she had seen a movie like that one time. The heroine can't carry a tune, then suddenly, at the climactic moment, when all eyes are upon her, she opens her mouth, and a beautiful nightingale's song pours forth.

Yet, facing grim reality, Dinah knew that Suzanne might still be the one to play Julie. Somehow the thought didn't tear her up inside the way the thought of Nick's being class president did. Maybe it was because she had lost a lead role to Suzanne once before, back in fifth grade, when Suzanne had been chosen over her to play Becky Thatcher in *The Adventures of Tom Sawyer*. Their friendship had survived, though it hadn't been easy. And now Dinah accepted occasional competition with Suzanne as a fact of life.

Why couldn't she be equally accepting of competition with Nick? Of course, she wasn't really *competing* with Nick for the office of class president. She had given up competing with anybody for anything. But how could *Nick* still go on striving, still go on caring about things, when the universe was going to end for him as surely as it was going to end for her? How could he go on when *she* wasn't going on? It seemed somehow disloyal for the boy who would have been her First Gentleman to make such a speedy switch to replacing her as president himself.

That night, Dinah's father wasn't home for dinner. His biology class met on Monday, Wednesday, and Friday nights, and this was the night of his first exam. So he had planned on grabbing a quick sandwich at the store and staying downtown to study.

Dinah used the evening to prepare herself for the voice auditions for *Carousel*, upstairs, alone in her room. She didn't actually sing "If I Loved You" out loud, because she didn't want her mother to hear her. But she sang it over and over again in her head, perfecting every nuance of feeling. She always began very quietly, in a cracked whisper. Then her voice built to a soaring crescendo as she finally faced the truth of her love. Finally, she imagined Nick, as Billy, singing the same song to her in reply. It was a very pleasant way to spend an evening.

Toward nine o'clock she drifted downstairs to find her mother.

"Daddy should be home soon," her mother said. "I hope he did well on his exam. I know he was worried about it."

Dinah sympathized. She took exams herself all the time, but this was the first exam her father had taken since he had left college twenty years ago.

"Here he is now," Dinah's mother said.

Dinah's father walked slowly into the family room. Dinah didn't have to ask him how the exam had gone; she knew the answer from the slump in his shoulders and the discouraged look about his eyes.

"Those young kids in my class tore out of there after less than an hour. I was writing up until the last possible minute, and I still didn't finish the darned thing."

"Do you think you passed?" Dinah's mother asked.

"Passed? As in got a D? Maybe. But I had been hoping for a bit more than that."

Dinah felt a lump in her throat. It was hard to imagine her grown-up father caring about something like grades, something that had mattered to Dinah last year, but that seemed unimportant now, in the face of all her new worries. But she loved her father so much that she couldn't bear to see him disappointed.

"You'll learn how to pace yourself better for the next one," Dinah's mother said, putting her arm around him.

Dinah had a sudden helpful thought. "When I take an exam, I go through first and answer all the questions I'm sure I know the answer to. Then I go back over the exam again and work more at the questions I didn't know the first time around. That way, if I run out of time, at least everything I've put down is right."

Her father drew her toward him for a kiss. "That is a very sensible plan," he said.

"You can be our back-to-school consultant," Dinah's mother told her. "You know more than either of us about how to do well on tests."

58

Dinah felt pleased at their praise. A voice audition was like a test. She only hoped she had somehow, miraculously, learned how to do well on that kind of test, too.

The voice auditions were held in the music room after school on Tuesday. Mr. Maurer, the music teacher, sat at the baby grand piano, playing for each student who came forward to sing. Over and over again, Dinah heard "If I Loved You." Some kids had good voices—loud, clear, and pleasant. Others sang too softly, or off key. But none of them were singing from the depths of their soul. Dinah could tell that the song didn't belong to any of them as it belonged to her, and to Nick.

"Dinah Seabrooke," Mrs. Bevens finally called.

Dinah took her place by the piano. She didn't need the score. She knew the song by heart.

She began to sing. Something was wrong. Dinah could hear that she was coming in on the wrong note. She broke off, and Mr. Maurer began the introduction again.

This time she was flat—or sharp? Somehow Dinah made herself go on, but now when the cracked whisper built to the soaring crescendo, it sounded so terrible that Dinah knew all too well that her silent practicing hadn't turned her into a world-famous opera star. She read the truth in Suzanne's eyes as she took her seat again.

"Suzanne Kelly."

Suzanne walked over to the piano and folded her hands in front of her. The piano began, and Suzanne joined in. The beautiful nightingale's voice that hadn't poured forth five minutes ago poured forth now.

If Dinah wasn't going to star in *Carousel*, maybe she could still be class president. It wasn't too late, in spite of everything. If she got her petition early enough on Wednesday, she could collect the needed twenty signatures by the end of the day. First period slipped by. Second period. On Dinah's poem, "In a Mere Five Billion Years," Ms. Dunne had written, "Profound thoughts!" Would it be betraying those profound thoughts to leap into a major presidential campaign? Dinah didn't know anymore.

Third period.

At the end of fourth period, Dinah stopped by the office.

"I'd like to pick up a petition," she told the school secretary.

"You know they're due this afternoon," the secretary said.

"I know."

Dinah still didn't plan to turn it in. She just wanted to look at it. "We, the undersigned, hereby nominate Dinah Seabrooke for the office of seventh-grade president." Even if she was going to renounce all earthly glory forever, it didn't hurt to imagine it one last time. And she really *would* be a wonderful class president. In some ways she would be even better than Blaine had been. Blaine was serious and sensible, but Dinah had drive and passion. She had a sudden fleeting vision of a new head carved on Mount Rushmore, a smaller, feminine head, with wild, curly, wind-blown hair.

She showed her petition to Suzanne at lunch, while Nick was away from the table getting another carton of milk.

"But I thought—" Suzanne looked confused. "I can't sign it. I already signed Nick's."

"That's okay," Dinah said. She wandered over to a couple of tables on the other side of the cafeteria to collect signatures, just in case. Eight kids signed. Eight down, twelve to go.

Sixth period passed. Three more kids signed. Seventh period. Dinah was up to sixteen signatures now. Those last four signatures were all that stood between her and a chance at Mount Rushmore. Four signatures—and Nick. It would be hard telling Nick that she had changed her mind and decided to run, after all. By now he was probably counting on being class president himself. But Dinah knew that Nick hadn't turned in his petition yet. He had waited until the end, as he had said he would.

Eighth period.

"Good afternoon, class," Mr. Mubashir said. "Today we will learn something about the birth of our own sun. Our sun's birthday came about five billion years ago. Our sun was born when a cloud of whirling gas, stirred up by the explosion of a distant supernova, gradually began to condense. . . ."

It all seemed heartbreakingly sad to Dinah, the birthday of one small, insignificant, out-of-the-way star, the star that was going to be the sun, *their* sun, live for a short ten billion years, and then consume itself and the very earth it had warmed and brightened.

Nick looked over at her. "Ocean-River?"

Dinah knew what the question meant. She shook her head. She couldn't do it. She couldn't. It would be like taking back everything she had felt inside for the last two weeks. Mount Rushmore itself was going to melt one day, the ageless profiles on the granite monument running together like molten wax, dripping from a sputtering candle.

"You're sure?"

Dinah nodded. Under her desk, she crumpled her petition into a small hard ball, like one of the two doomed moons of Mars.

Seven

So Dinah wasn't going to star in *Carousel* or be class president. It was odd to think that just a couple of weeks ago she had been making plans about what kind of footprints she was going to leave behind her on the sands of time.

Of course she could still be a champion debater and leave a few small, fleeting footprints that way. Last year she had promised Mr. Dixon that she would be on JFK's brand-new debate team, which he was in the process of forming. She couldn't back out of the promise now, however much she felt like backing out of everything.

Besides, Dinah loved debating. She almost loved it more than acting. She had debated against Nick back in sixth grade, in Mr. Dixon's social studies class, on the topic of capital punishment. Dinah had argued for capital punishment, and Nick had argued against it. Dinah had stopped hating Nick the very same moment that Nick had convinced her to stop supporting capital punishment. But this year, Dinah wasn't going to be debating *against* Nick. She and Nick were going to be partners, debating together against other teams.

The first debate-team meeting was held after school that day. Nick turned in his petition on the way. Dinah stood by his side as he did it, smiling a too-bright First Lady smile.

The middle-school debate team was small, just four seventh graders and four eighth graders, hand-picked by Mr. Dixon. Dinah didn't know the other two seventh graders: a boy named Scott Martin and a girl named Lin Lee. She gave them a pitying appraisal, as she and Nick took seats together toward the front of the room. Lin and Scott both looked smart, but hardly a match for Nick and Dinah.

Mr. Dixon banged on his desk to get their attention. "Debaters!" he boomed jovially, his voice as loud as if there had been a hundred students in the room instead of eight. "I hope your killer instincts have had a chance to develop over the summer."

Dinah glanced at Scott and Lin again. They didn't look very threatening to her. Neither did Nick, for that matter, though Dinah knew from firsthand experience that he liked to win. And so did she. When they had competed against each other, this had been a source of tension. But now, as they competed together, on the same side, debating should form another bond between them, maybe one strong enough to make up for the election.

Mr. Dixon explained how the debate team would operate. They would debate the same issue all year long. Mr. Dixon didn't say what this year's issue would be. Instead he told them about the extensive research they would need to do, to prepare themselves to argue both sides of the issue. Debaters didn't find out which side they were arguing until they arrived at a meet.

Mr. Dixon went on to explain that they would have a few practice debates early in the fall among themselves. Then they would begin competing against teams from other schools.

He still hadn't announced the topic. Dinah's mind was racing. If only it were capital punishment. Nobody on earth would be able to defeat Dinah and Nick on capital punishment. Or maybe it would have something to do with the environment, maybe even with recycling. Dinah didn't know if she could argue *against* recycling, but she could certainly argue *for* it at a moment's notice.

"Our debate topic for this academic year is . . ." Mr. Dixon turned to write on the board. "Resolved: That the U.S. government should substantially strengthen regulation of immigration to the United States."

Disappointment struck Dinah like a blow. Was Mr. Dixon joking? She had no idea whether the government should substantially strengthen regulation of immigration. She had never spent one single minute of her life pondering immigration policy. How could she debate such a boring topic for a whole entire year?

Dinah looked over at Nick, but he was busy copying the topic into his notebook. So were Lin and Scott. Dinah copied it into her notebook, too. But in her heart she knew that she had as good a chance of winning a debate trophy as she had had of singing "If I Loved You" on key. And if she and Nick failed as debate partners, it would be hard not to see that as an omen for their relationship. Then Dinah would have neither play nor presidency, neither debating fame nor . . . Nick.

After school, Dinah hurried off to Mrs. Briscoe's house. There was no one like Mrs. Briscoe when Dinah was feeling miserable. Dinah would make her try to guess the debate topic. Mrs. Briscoe would give up after a few tries, and then Dinah would give an imitation of Mr. Dixon making the announcement, and the two of them could laugh about it together.

Dinah rang Mrs. Briscoe's bell, but Mrs. Briscoe didn't answer. At first Dinah was puzzled—Mrs. Briscoe never went anywhere in the afternoon—and then afraid. Once, last year, Mrs. Briscoe hadn't come to the door when Dinah knocked, and it turned out that she had fallen on the stairs and broken her leg. Mrs. Briscoe had heart problems, too. Dinah's own heart clenched inside her chest. If anything ever happened to Mrs. Briscoe . . .

But then the door finally opened. Dinah's knees felt weak with relief.

"Come in, Dinah! Come in!" Mrs. Briscoe said. "I'm ashamed to admit it, but I was taking the tiniest bit of a nap."

"Should I come back some other time?" Dinah asked, hoping desperately that Mrs. Briscoe would say no.

"No, no, not at all. A nice pot of tea is just what I need to wake up."

Dinah followed Mrs. Briscoe to her kitchen, down a long hallway made more narrow by the stacks of yellowing newspapers lining one side. A year ago Dinah's mother had been given the job, in her organization consulting business, of organizing Mrs. Briscoe's astonishingly disorganized house. Dinah had helped her mother bundle up hundreds of piles of newspapers for the recycling center. Now the newspaper piles were creeping back again.

First Dinah told Mrs. Briscoe all about the election and *Carousel*. She had found in the past that when she told stories about sad things that had happened to her, the sadness in the stories began to disappear and they became just—stories. And Dinah took satisfaction in knowing that her stories were always especially humorous and engaging.

"*Carousel* is a wonderful show," Mrs. Briscoe agreed. "Those songs! I can't hear 'You'll Never Walk Alone' without breaking down like a baby. Suzanne will make a splendid Julie. And it sounds like your Nick will make a fine class president."

"They will," Dinah said, forgiving Mrs. Briscoe for the compliments. "But—I wish I could sing. I mean, I really thought that maybe I could sing, just because I wanted to so much."

"You were very brave to try," Mrs. Briscoe said. "When I look back on my life, I find that the only things I'm really sorry for now are the times I *didn't* try."

Dinah thought that over for a minute. Maybe that was another reason why she felt worse about the election than about the play. She hadn't even tried to be class president. But it had seemed so pointless to try.

"The debate team met today," Dinah said then. "Guess what this year's topic is."

"Oh, I'm sure I don't have any idea," Mrs. Briscoe said.

"Just guess." Dinah smiled expectantly. How Mrs. Briscoe would hoot when she heard the topic Mr. Dixon had finally written on the board.

"Well, let me see. I would think that welfare reform would be an exciting topic. Or maybe something to do with immigration policy."

Dinah was stunned. "That *is* the topic: immigration. You think it's *interesting*? I thought it was boring."

"Certainly not!" Mrs. Briscoe said. "I must have seen a dozen articles on immigration in the past few months. And isn't it a lucky thing that I've been saving the papers! I had a hunch they would come in handy."

"It doesn't sound *boring*?" Dinah asked again. " 'The U.S. government should substantially strengthen regulation of immigration'?"

"It won't be when *you're* debating it," Mrs. Briscoe said. "Let's each take a pair of scissors and start going through these papers. And when we're done, maybe I'll send them off for recycling."

Dinah began the hunt for scissors, for nothing in Mrs. Briscoe's house was ever where Mrs. Briscoe thought it was. She felt a faint surge of hope. She would do her best on the debate team this year. And she would keep trying in her relationship with Nick.

Dinah's father picked her up from Mrs. Briscoe's on his way home from work.

"I guess we'll get back our exams tonight," he told her on the ride home. "It'll be good to find out exactly which questions I got wrong. And I'm going to talk to the professor after class and see if I can get her to give me any tips on how to study better."

Dinah couldn't help asking a question. "Do you ever wonder—I mean, do you really think going back to school is worth all the trouble?"

"Sure," her father said. "I'm tired of the store, honey. My job there is something I just drifted into, after I got out of the Navy. It was never what I really *wanted* to do. And now that I'm forty, I want to make sure I find what I really do enjoy doing before it's too late."

Dinah needed to clarify her question. "But whether you find it or not, I mean, you're just going to die in the end, anyway."

"Whoa!"

To her surprise, Dinah's father pulled over to the side of the road and turned off the ignition. "This sounds pretty serious. Is it connected to all that moaning and groaning about the sun we heard a couple of weeks ago?"

"Uh-huh."

"Honey, it's *because* I'm going to die someday that I want to make my life now the best I possibly can. I don't want to be seventy, eighty, ninety, and feel that I never really *lived*."

"But what *difference* does it make, in the end?"

"It makes a difference," her father said. "It makes a difference to me."

But *why*? Dinah didn't bother asking. She knew he wouldn't be able to tell her, any more than she could tell him why she couldn't stop feeling the way she did.

"Is everything all right at school?" her father asked then. "We haven't heard any stories lately. Your mom and I worry when we don't hear stories from you. Though most of the time your stories make us worry, too."

"Everything's all right at school," Dinah said. Except for the election, and the play, and the debate team. But for some reason, she didn't feel like telling sad stories to her parents anymore. She told them only to Mrs. Briscoe.

"And with Nick?"

"And with Nick." Sort of.

Dinah's father didn't look satisfied, but he turned the engine on and steered the car back into the slow line of rush-hour traffic, all those cars creeping forward in the twilight toward wherever it was they were trying to go.

Eight

Mrs. Briscoe was right, as usual. The more Dinah read about immigration policy, the more interesting it became. Right away, Dinah felt herself in sympathy with the negative—that the government should welcome immigration, not restrict it. After all, the United States was a nation of immigrants. If poor people desperate for a way out of poverty or oppression couldn't come to America, where *could* they go? The challenge was to make herself come up with powerful arguments for the other side. Though whether or not they were able to immigrate to the United States, everybody in the world was going to die in the end, anyway.

Dinah wrote a poem on the topic for Ms. Dunne. It was called "A Few Thoughts on Immigration Policy":

The Haitian refugees who wait for asylum may get
   it; but they will still die.

The undocumented Mexican workers who cross the
　　border into Texas may find jobs, but they will still
　　die.
The Vietnamese immigrants who own the corner
　　convenience store, and the Korean immigrants who
　　work in the filling station, and the Taiwanese
　　immigrants who work at the pharmacy will all
　　die.
The tired, the poor, the huddled masses yearning to
　　breathe free—all will die someday, whatever it
　　says on the Statue of Liberty.
Illegal aliens, legal aliens, United States citizens—all
　　will die.
Everybody will die.

Dinah read it over, pleased. From the title through
to the last line, it was her best poem to date.

Dinah had been writing a lot of haiku, too. Ms.
Dunne adored haiku. Haiku was a Japanese style of
nature poetry. A haiku was very short, just three
lines, with five syllables in the first line, seven in the
second, and five in the third. Dinah would find herself in the middle of doing something else, and then
the idea for a haiku would just come to her, like a
special, sudden, unexpected gift. Once she had the
idea, it was a lot of work to make all the syllables
come out right, but it was a wonderful kind of work
—like solving an extremely challenging and complicated puzzle that turned out to be a tiny seventeen-
syllable treasure.

One golden leaf falls
From the maple in my yard—
Soon all leaves will die.

In the evenings now
There is just a hint of frost—
Icy death to come.

Birds are flying south.
Don't they know that death can come
To the south as well?

At least Dinah could still write poetry. She was grateful
for that.

Nick was busy with his campaign. At Dinah's suggestion, he had decided to base his candidacy on environmental issues. His campaign slogan was "Nick
Tribble: The Next Step." The idea was that Blaine's
recycling program was the first step, and the great environmental programs that Nick would launch would
be the next step. All Nick's posters were green, to carry
out the environmental theme.

Dinah helped Nick make the posters on Sunday evening. She helped him think of catchy things to write
on them, like: "Save more trees? Vote Tribble, please!"
and "Even WORMS know where it's at: Vote Tribble!"
The worm poster showed cute little worm heads poking
up out of the JFK Middle School compost heap, where
all food waste from the cafeteria would turn into dark,

fertile, nitrogen-rich soil once Nick was elected president. Dinah was the one who drew the worm heads. And then before the first bell on Monday, Dinah helped Nick tape up his posters all over the halls at school.

"Maybe we could hang one in some really crazy place, like outside on the big sign in front of the school," Nick suggested.

"I did that last year," Dinah informed him. "Roemer made me take it down." Nick hadn't been around for Dinah's campaign in sixth grade, because his family hadn't moved to Riverdale until the spring.

"Or maybe I could do some kind of stunt or something. Like pile a big heap of food waste outside of Roemer's office."

"I did that, too," Dinah said, trying to keep the note of impatience out of her voice. "Not food waste, but trash. I filled a bunch of trash bags with all the paper in everybody's wastebaskets and dragged them all through the school."

"Or—there must be something else I could do, something that would really get everyone's attention."

"I wore a recycling bucket to school on my head."

"You did?" Nick finally sounded impressed.

"But it didn't work out. It kind of backfired. Everyone just started calling me Bucket Head."

"Yeah, but they remembered who you were. My dad says there's no such thing as bad publicity. There must be something else we can do."

Dinah tuned out; she had no suggestions to offer. Other people's campaigns, she was finding out, weren't much more interesting than other people's vacations in England. There was a definite limit to what Dinah was willing to do to speed Nick on the way to seventh-grade fame and glory.

Toward the end of the fourth week of class, Ms. Dunne gave Dinah back her copy of "A Few Thoughts on Immigration Policy." On the bottom, the teacher had written: "Please come and see me. Are you free after eighth period today?"

Why would Ms. Dunne want to see her? Dinah felt a pleasurable tingle of anticipation. It had to be something good, like a nationwide poetry contest for Dinah to enter, or the announcement of a new magazine that published poetry by extremely gifted seventh graders. Or maybe Ms. Dunne just wanted to discuss ways in which she could work with Dinah outside of class to develop her unusual poetic gifts.

As soon as the bell rang at the end of eighth period, Dinah hurried to Ms. Dunne's room. The teacher smiled as Dinah poked her head in the doorway, but her smile was less bright than her classroom smiles.

"Sit down, Dinah," Ms. Dunne said.

Mystified now, Dinah took her usual seat, in the second row.

"Dinah, you've been writing some very nice poems for me this fall, but I wonder—lately, they're all on the same topic."

"Death," Dinah said, trying not to sound too smug. She knew that the other seventh graders weren't writing poems as dark and powerful as hers, on such a serious and important topic. They were still writing little sing-song poems about their pets.

Ms. Dunne leaned closer to Dinah, her face soft with concern. "Dinah, has anyone close to you died recently? Or is someone dying?"

"No," Dinah said, taken aback at the question.

"No?" Ms. Dunne asked gently.

Dinah began to feel embarrassed as the teacher waited patiently for her reply. What was she supposed to say? Was someone dying? *Everyone* was dying, including Dinah herself. But if Ms. Dunne hadn't noticed that yet, it didn't seem Dinah's place to point it out, particularly since she had already pointed it out as clearly as possible in "A Few Thoughts on Immigration Policy."

"No," Dinah repeated, swallowing back her disap-pointment. Apparently Ms. Dunne wasn't going to sug-gest that Dinah enter "A Few Thoughts" in a poetry contest or rush it off for immediate publication.

"Well, anyway, Dinah, I just wanted you to know that I'm here if you ever need to talk. And I wanted to remind you that we have a fine psychologist here at JFK Middle School, Ms. Isenberg."

"Okay," Dinah said, relieved that the conversation seemed to be over. She stood up to go.

Hundreds of poets before Dinah had written poems about death. The seventh-grade reader was full of fa-mous poems about death, by Shakespeare, Dylan Thomas, Emily Dickinson. Had anyone ever suggested to Shakespeare and Emily Dickinson that they might want to visit their school psychologist? A person wasn't crazy for caring about death. It would have been crazier *not* to care.

At the first practice debate, held after school on Wednesday of the following week, Dinah and Nick debated Lin and Scott. Nick and Dinah argued against restricting immigration; Lin and Scott argued for it. Dinah was almost crying as she portrayed the squalor of Third World slums in which starving children begged for crusts of bread. Nick was calm and reasonable as he pointed out the numerous benefits that immigrant workers brought to the U.S. economy. It seemed to Dinah that they complemented each other perfectly.

But Lin and Scott won the debate. Lin and Scott just had so many *facts*. Dinah didn't see how their brains could have room left over for anything else once all those facts about immigration policy had been crammed in. It was obvious that Lin and Scott had worked enormously hard over the past two weeks, far harder than Nick and Dinah had worked.

"You two did very well," Mr. Dixon told Nick and Dinah after he announced their losing score. "But all the emotion in the world doesn't have the impact of one well-chosen statistic."

Dinah took that as directed at her personally. *She* had been the one who had shown emotion during the debate, not Nick. Her cheeks burned as she remembered how her voice had cracked when she had talked about the starving babies. Mr. Dixon might as well have come right out and said that Nick had done better in the debate than Dinah had. But Nick hadn't spouted statistics, either. His brain was no more stuffed with facts than hers was. And Dinah had so many really *big* facts to keep track of these days, from Mr. Mubashir's class. She couldn't keep track of everything.

For a few moments, as they walked together in silence toward the bus, Dinah thought Nick was going to have the good sense not to say anything. But then he said, "Emotion, huh. I guess from now on, we'll have to tone down the dramatics a bit."

He said *we*, but Dinah knew he meant *you*. Nick hadn't had any "dramatics" in his speech.

"It's not as if you had any great facts, either," Dinah blurted out.

Nick looked surprised. "Well, I guess I haven't spent as much time in the library as I meant to. I've been pretty busy these days, running my campaign."

The election was still a sore point with Dinah. Every time she saw a green poster in the hall, a tiny voice inside her shrieked "Copy Cat!" It seemed to her as if Nick had made the same posters she would have made and then crossed out her name and written in his. Dinah felt crossed out. Crossed out of *Carousel*, crossed out of the election, and now crossed out of debate, as well.

Dinah knew that she shouldn't say anything else, not when she was feeling so hurt and angry inside, but, sure enough, she heard herself say, "Oh, the *election*. Well. We wouldn't want anything to interfere with your *election*."

"What's wrong with you?" Nick asked. "So we lost one debate. Big deal."

"Nothing," Dinah said. "There's nothing to be *emotional* about, is there. People may be so desperately poor that they will sell their own children so they won't have to watch them starve to death, but we shouldn't get *dramatic* about it, now, should we?"

"Mr. Dixon was the one who said you were too emotional, not me."

Ah-ha. Now it was *you*. Dinah had known the *we* couldn't last too long. Had she ever really thought she and Nick were too alike? They were too different. Dinah *cared* about things, like the plight of starving refugees and the burning out of the sun. Nick didn't. He wasn't emotional, and she was. That was all there was to it. A line from *Gone With the Wind* suddenly echoed in Dinah's mind: Scarlett O'Hara's father telling her, "Like must marry like, or there'll be no happiness." There was certainly no happiness for Dinah and Nick.

"Fine!" Dinah said brightly. "Don't worry. I won't inflict my *emotions* on you anymore."

Nick got on the bus and sat on an empty seat toward the front. Dinah made a point of walking past him as if he were invisible, less than invisible, an infinitesimal speck of cosmic dust.

Nine

That was that. It seemed only fitting and proper for Dinah to be once more done with Nick forever. She took a melancholy satisfaction in mentally crossing him off her seventh-grade list. Now she had no lead in the play, no class office, no debate victory, and no boyfriend. There was something grimly pleasing about such a clean sweep of all her hopes and dreams.

Dinah wrote a poem about it at home that evening.

The Null Set

I have nothing.
Nothing.
No thing.
My life is a set
Without any members

As empty as
A solar system
Without any sun.

The poem was another masterpiece. Moreover, it showed that Dinah could integrate learning across the curriculum: They had studied null sets in Ms. Lewis's math class. But Dinah knew better now than to show the poem to Ms. Dunne. It would only make her worry.

Nick didn't call. Dinah hadn't thought he would.

The next day was the seventh-grade election assembly, held third period in the middle-school gym. Each candidate for class office gave a two-minute speech. Dinah had to admit that Nick gave by far the best speech of the three presidential candidates, filled with enough environmental facts to impress even Mr. Dixon. But she refused to let her heart melt. It was easy to give a good speech when you had copied all the ideas in it from your former, overly emotional girlfriend.

The election took place the following day, Friday. Students voted in their homerooms; the results would be announced over the PA system at the end of eighth period.

Dinah quickly checked the boxes she wanted for secretary, treasurer, and vice president. Then she stared down at the three names for class president:

Eliza Evans
Nicholas Tribble
Jason Winfield

There was space to add a write-in candidate. Dinah thought of printing in her own name, or Blaine's. Or she could just leave that whole section of the ballot blank. Or she could vote for Eliza Evans. At least Eliza was a girl. But Eliza's campaign platform had been dumb—something about better teacher-student relations.

Finally Dinah picked up her pen and put the smallest possible check mark next to Nick's name. She hoped that whoever was counting the votes had a magnifying glass handy.

"Ocean-River." Nick touched her arm in the hall as she was walking to first period.

Dinah almost relented. Nick's fingers on her arm felt so gentle and warm. But if there was no future with Nick, if she and Nick were really too different for their relationship to work out over the long term, why prolong what would only turn out to be the agony of parting?

Dinah jerked her arm away. "Don't worry, I voted for you," she said coldly.

Nick quickly extinguished the questioning look in his eyes. "Good, good!" he said, as if that had been all he wanted to know. "Keep those votes coming in, folks! Vote early and often. Tribble's in the White House, waiting to be elected. Winfield's in the garbage can, waiting to be collected!"

Jason, overhearing him, gave Nick a friendly punch in the arm, and the two rivals fell into step together. Dinah walked the rest of the way to math class alone.

Mrs. Briscoe's favorite song from *Carousel* had been "You'll Never Walk Alone." Ha! True poets often walked alone, composing soul-stirring poetry in their heads.

At the start of eighth period, Mr. Mubashir rubbed his hands together with pleasure. His face beamed like the classroom model of the sun, lit from within by a small yellow light bulb.

"Ladies and gentlemen!" he said. "I have some news for you, good news!"

Dinah looked up from her book. She had been busy inking over the little lacy hearts she had drawn on the brown-paper cover of her science book a week ago, with "D.S. + N.T." printed neatly inside each one. Now she was scribbling over the hearts so hard that her ballpoint pen ripped through the brown paper. Good news? It had been a long time since Dinah had heard any news that could qualify as good.

"Next week, on Friday, we will go on our first class trip, to the Air and Space Museum! You will have to miss your other classes, I am afraid."

Loud applause.

"But I have assured your teachers that this will be an important learning experience for you."

As Mr. Mubashir passed out the permission slips, he told the class more about the trip. They would leave JFK Middle School right after homeroom and return at four-thirty. They would see a special astronomy exhibit. They would view a movie about the space program shown on a screen seven stories high. Weather permitting, they would have a picnic outside on the huge outdoor mall in Washington, D.C.

"Are there any questions?" Mr. Mubashir asked.

"Can we sit with whoever we want to on the bus?" someone asked.

"Yes, yes!" Mr. Mubashir said.

"What are you going to do if Artie throws up on the bus like he did when we went to Annapolis last year?"

Mr. Mubashir's smile began to fade, as if the light bulb inside his head had a dimmer switch. "Does anyone have any questions about the *museum*? No? Then let us turn in our books to the problems at the end of Chapter Two."

Dinah felt excited in spite of herself. A class trip was just what she needed to take her mind off her troubles. Anything could happen on a class trip. Some kind of adventure was practically guaranteed. And travel was good for a poet. It was bound to provide new subject matter for a poem.

A few minutes before the end of eighth period, the PA system in Mr. Mubashir's room clicked on, and Mr. Roemer cleared his throat.

"Attention, students. The vote tally for this year's class elections is now complete. Our new class officers are: For eighth-grade president, Rose Compton . . ."

Dinah dug her fingernails into her palm, waiting for the seventh-grade results. Did she hope that Nick would win or that he would lose?

". . . For seventh-grade president, Nicholas Tribble . . ."

The class waited quietly until the other seventh-grade officers had been announced, then erupted into cheers. Jason's chin was set a bit too high, but he quickly extended his hand to Nick. The other boys pounded Nick on the back, and the girls crowded around him, too. The closing bell rang, but nobody paid any attention to it.

At first Dinah held back, but it would be childish not to offer Nick her congratulations, at least. If Jason could shake Nick's hand, so could she. Dinah forced her way into the throng surrounding Nick and stuck out her hand. Nick shook it as if it were a stranger's hand, and then he shook another hand, and another, and another.

It could have been Dinah's hand that everyone was shaking. But it wasn't. Dinah wasn't president, for the second year in a row, and she wasn't First Lady, either. In the long run—the really long run, the five-billion-year long run—it wouldn't matter. But first Dinah had to get through the short run. Her chest pounded with a mixture of jealousy, yearning, and stiff, sore pride. Quietly she slipped out of the room and hurried to her locker, knowing that none of the others would even notice that she was gone.

The weekend loomed before Dinah, an endless stretch of hours, minutes, and seconds to be filled. The one thing she was *not* going to do was walk down Nick's street and look at his house. She wasn't even going to *consider* doing that.

Friday night, Dinah read in her room. The book was

Wuthering Heights, and it was wonderful. Dinah stayed up past midnight to finish it. The story of Heathcliff and Catherine's doomed love suited Dinah perfectly. Catherine and Heathcliff were alike in their stormy, passionate natures, but they came to each other from worlds that were too different. At least Catherine hadn't had to deal with Heathcliff's being triumphantly elected class president two days after they had parted.

If only Dinah lived on a storm-tossed moor! The bright sunshine pouring through her window on Saturday morning seemed particularly inappropriate.

After breakfast, Dinah watched her father study for a while; his second biology exam was only a week away. It was fascinating to see her father—her regular grown-up father—taking notes in his notebook as if he were a seventh grader.

"You know, honey, studying is not the kind of thing I do better with an audience," her father said after a few minutes.

Dinah herself did everything better with an audience, but she turned to go. The last thing she wanted to do was distract her father from a project that meant so much to him.

She found her mother upstairs, organizing a bureau drawer. Benjamin sat on the floor next to her, building tall towers of Duplos and knocking them down.

"Everyone thinks an organization consultant has a perfectly organized house," her mother said. "It's a good thing they don't come over and look in my drawers."

"The newspaper piles at Mrs. Briscoe's house are getting pretty big again," Dinah told her. Up went another Duplo tower; down it came again.

"I figured they would. Most people can change only so much. I expect that if I dropped in on most of my clients a year later, I'd find that their lives were pretty much the way they were before I ever came."

"But . . ." Dinah tried to be tactful. "Then doesn't organizing them seem—you know—kind of a big waste?"

Her mother shrugged. "Most of what we do every day has to be done over again the next day. Eating, sleeping, cleaning, changing Benjamin's diapers. That's just how life is. Look at it this way. It's good for my business. It keeps my customers coming back. What are your plans for today, sweetie?"

"I don't have any. I guess I'll go over to Suzanne's for a while. Or maybe I'll go see Mrs. Briscoe."

Benjamin finished building another Duplo tower, his tallest yet. He laughed out loud when he sent the small plastic blocks sprawling. Some people apparently were not bothered by the utter uselessness of their activities.

"You and Nick still haven't made up this time?" Dinah's mother asked.

"No," Dinah said. And this time they weren't going to, either.

As Dinah knocked on Suzanne's door, she heard Suzanne playing one of the songs from *Carousel* on the piano.

After all, Dinah had ended up getting a small part in the play, the part of Enoch Snow's obnoxious daughter. It was actually a pretty good part, for a role that had only two lines total.

"Do you know your lines yet?" Dinah asked Suzanne as the girls settled down to share a bag of M&Ms in the kitchen.

"Most of them. I think. Or a lot of them." Suzanne twisted the end of one of her long blond braids, the way she sometimes did when she wasn't sure of something.

"Do you want me to practice with you?" Dinah felt saintly unselfishness radiating out from her like a halo.

Suzanne's face brightened. "Sure! If you wouldn't mind. I have my script right here."

Then Suzanne hesitated. "Did you—have you talked to Nick since the election?"

"No," Dinah said shortly. "Why?"

"No reason. Just—Greg is coming over to watch videos tonight, and I thought you and Nick might like to come, too, if—"

"Forget it," Dinah said, her halo of saintliness fading. Suzanne and Greg had always had a nice, easy, uncomplicated relationship. Unlike Dinah and Nick, who now had no relationship at all. "Let's just read lines, okay?"

"Okay," Suzanne said, her eyes troubled.

Dinah started reading at the top of Act One, trying her best to keep her voice from trembling.

———

When Dinah rang Mrs. Briscoe's bell later that afternoon, her daughter, Ruth, answered the door. Dinah swallowed back her disappointment. She had met Ruth Briscoe a few times and didn't like her very much. Ruth Briscoe always gave the impression that she was in a big hurry to do something much more important than interact with her mother, or with her mother's twelve-year-old friend.

"Oh, it's you, Dinah," Ruth Briscoe said. She didn't ask Dinah to come in.

"Is your mother at home?" Dinah asked stiffly.

"She's here, but we're visiting right now, and after I leave she's going to need to rest. Her heart's been bothering her this week. Why don't you come back tomorrow?"

"Okay," Dinah said. But she didn't want to talk to Mrs. Briscoe *tomorrow*. She wanted to talk to her *now*, this very minute.

Ruth Briscoe shut the door. And for the first time since the debate loss, the breakup with Nick, and Nick's election, Dinah found herself wiping away tears.

Ten
___

Friday morning after homeroom, Dinah hurried outside to board the bus for the Air and Space Museum. It was a gray, gloomy morning, with a raw edge to the wind. Dinah scuffled through a drift of fallen leaves blown across the sidewalk in front of JFK Middle School. Even if you had no boyfriend, and the boy who wasn't your boyfriend was class president, there was nothing more satisfying than walking ankle-deep in dry, crackling leaves on your way to a bus bound for a full day's class trip.

Dinah and Suzanne sat together, toward the front of the bus, and Nick and Artie sat together, toward the back. Dinah and Nick hadn't spoken to each other all week. They should have been working together as hard as they could in preparation for the next practice debate, but Dinah cared more about not speaking to an enemy than she did about not losing a debate. Apparently, Nick felt the same way. And if they did speak to each other, what would they say? Would they just sit side by side at a table in the library, politely chatting about immigration policy, as if they hadn't kissed each other so many times that Dinah had finally lost count?

The bus ride into Washington took over an hour. By the time the great white dome of the Capitol came into view, Suzanne knew every last one of Julie's lines from *Carousel*, and the pound-size bag of M&M's Dinah had brought for the trip was empty. Once everyone was off the bus, Mr. Mubashir lined the students up two by two to enter the museum. Somehow it turned out that Nick and Artie were directly behind Dinah and Suzanne.

Still holding her crumpled M&M bag, Dinah looked around for a trash can. Suddenly a gust of wind blew the wrapper from her hand and sent it sailing across the street.

"Dinah *littered*!" Artie called out, loudly enough that everyone in front of them in line turned around to stare. "Oh, Mr. Environmental President, sir, I just saw Dinah litter!"

Annoyed, Dinah darted out of line to catch the wrapper. Nick beat her to it. Dinah didn't say anything as Nick dropped the wrapper in a trash can. He hadn't done it for *her*; the environmental president couldn't very well watch a piece of litter waft by without doing *something*.

"I wouldn't do the jitterbug, With a lousy litterbug,"

Artie sang, still at full volume. "Too bad Ms. Dunne's not here. This is the best poem I've written since school started. Let's see. Here's some more. It's really a disaster, When someone drops a wrapper. I'm glad it's not my job, To clean up after slobs."

"I didn't *drop* it," Dinah snapped. "It just blew. Besides, *disaster* doesn't rhyme with *wrapper*. And *job* doesn't rhyme with *slobs*."

"Close enough," Artie said.

As the JFK group filed into the museum, Artie kept on chanting lines about litterbugs and jitterbugs. It was beginning to get on Dinah's nerves. At least when the sun burned itself out there wouldn't be any more Arties.

The special exhibit on astronomy turned out to be fascinating. One case held some fragments of moon rocks—actual rocks brought back by astronauts over twenty-five years before from the surface of the moon. Dinah wished the case were open so she could touch one with her bare hand. A short film on comets played on a small built-in TV.

Then, on a table in the second room of the exhibit, Dinah saw a stack of fliers. She glanced at the top one: "Have a star named after you!" The flier went on to say that if you sent in a check for twenty-five dollars you could have a star named after you, a real star that no one had ever named before.

Dinah felt a powerful yearning: her very own star! She could put in a request for a super-young star, a baby star just one or two billion years old. That way, even after their sun burned out, she could sort of keep on going.

"Suzanne!" Dinah called. She handed Suzanne a flier. "We can have stars named after us. We could get two right next to each other: a Dinah Seabrooke star and a Suzanne Kelly star."

Suzanne shook her head. "Twenty-five dollars is a lot of money. And it's not as if they can stick a label on the star. They'll just write it down in some book somewhere that no one will even read."

"Still," Dinah said. "They'd be stars that nobody in the world ever named before, and they'd be named after us."

Suzanne looked doubtful.

"Twinkle, twinkle, Dinah Seabrooke," Dinah recited dreamily, tucking the flier in the pocket of her backpack. "I'm going to do it. I'll ask my parents if I can earn some extra money baby-sitting for Benjamin. It's worth it."

"I'll just look at your star," Suzanne said. "I don't think both of us need stars."

The next room contained a series of scales you could stand on to see what you would weigh on different planets, and on the moon. The larger the planet, the greater its gravitational force, and the more your weight. Dinah, who weighed a hundred and three pounds on earth, would weigh only seventeen pounds on the moon, but she would weigh three hundred pounds on Jupiter.

She tried to hop off each scale quickly, so no one

else would see what she weighed. A person's weight was her own private business. But naturally, Artie and Nick were right behind her as she stepped off the Jupiter scale.

"Dinah weighs three hundred pounds!" Artie shouted. "I just thought of another poem. This must be my poetic day. Here it goes: Dinah weighs three hundred pounds. She can't get any fatter. If she was playing Santa Claus, We wouldn't have to pad her."

Dinah felt her cheeks flame. Usually she didn't mind teasing. She even liked it. But lately nothing in her life was the way it usually was. She was conscious of the slight bulge in her stomach where her share of the pound bag of M&M's had settled. If she had it to do over again, she wouldn't have eaten quite so many. Even the thought of her very own star wasn't as cheering as it had been ten minutes ago. Dinah's star might burn on after the sun burned out, but there would be nobody to *know* it was Dinah's star burning. There would be no one to see it twinkle or to make a wish upon it.

"I thought of a better one," Nick said. "Dinah weighs three hundred pounds. She can't get any fatter. The earth is round instead of flat. But where she stands, it's flatter."

The traitor! To think she had once let him think he was her boyfriend! If she hadn't hated Nick before, she hated him now.

Dinah knew she should snap back with a funny poem

of her own. But Dinah wasn't good at writing funny poems these days. She hated herself for the sudden, self-pitying tears that stung her eyes.

Nick looked over at her curiously as he stepped on the Jupiter scale. Dinah didn't wait to snicker at what he weighed. She turned around and walked away, back through the first room of the solar system exhibit and out into the museum's gigantic exhibit hall. She wished she could climb into the rocket ship on display and blast into outer space, never to return.

"Dinah!"

She heard Nick calling her. Quickly Dinah slipped over to the line of people waiting to climb up into the rocket ship. She hid herself behind a tall, broad-shouldered tourist. Peeking out from behind the man's large tote bag, Dinah saw Nick hurrying in the other direction looking for her. Let him look! It was one thing for him to have teased her in the days when he still liked her. It was another thing for him to tease her now, with Artie.

Dinah's turn to enter the rocket ship came just as Nick retraced his steps past the exhibit. She slipped inside before he could see her. By the time she emerged from the space capsule, he was gone.

Now what? Dinah knew she should quietly go back to the solar system exhibit and rejoin her class, pretending she had never left. But she couldn't bear it. She wouldn't be able to pretend she had never left, anyway; obviously, Nick had noticed that she was gone. So there would be a new round of supposedly humorous poems from Nick and Artie about how she had run away, how she couldn't take a joke.

Dinah decided to wait for a while in the museum cafeteria, until she felt ready to go back. Just as she was entering the cafeteria, she saw Nick coming out.

For a fleeting moment their eyes met.

Dinah ran.

Nick pounded after her, through the cafeteria and then out again.

"No running in the museum!" a uniformed guard called. Dinah didn't listen.

Nick was a faster runner than Dinah, but Dinah had enough of a head start to leap onto the up escalator well ahead of Nick, so that by the time he stepped on, there were a dozen people crowded between them. She was halfway across the long second-floor hall before he could reach the top. Then, as he was closing in on her, Dinah tore past her rocket ship again and hurled herself into a waiting elevator just before its doors drew together. Downstairs again, Dinah pelted past the old-time airplanes.

"No running in the museum!" a second guard called to her. Dinah streaked by. Across the lobby she sprinted, sensing Nick behind her. She'd head outside and run all the way to the top of the Washington Monument.

"No running in the museum!" The third guard caught Dinah by the arm, caught her and held her fast. "What do you think you're doing?" he demanded. "This is a museum, not an indoor track. Where are your parents?"

Struggling to catch her breath, Dinah scowled across the lobby. Nick saw her and slowed to a walk.

"Your parents," the guard repeated. "Where are they?"

"I'm not here with my *parents*," Dinah said coldly. "I'm here with my school."

"Which school?" With his free hand, the guard fumbled for his pocket notepad, as if to write her a ticket for running in the museum.

Dinah didn't answer. Then, over the museum's booming PA system, she heard, "Dinah Seabrooke. Nicholas Tribble. Please rejoin your school group at the Jefferson Drive entrance to the museum."

"That you?" the guard asked.

Dinah nodded wearily. But she felt a small stirring of satisfaction. She had known something exciting would happen on the class trip; she hadn't known that her name would be broadcast throughout the whole vast museum.

Sternly the guard led Dinah to the other entrance to the museum; Nick trailed behind. Mr. Mubashir came striding across the lobby to meet them, relief flashing in his dark eyes.

"Dinah! Nick!" The guard let go of Dinah's arm. "We must all stay together. This museum is a very large place. From now on, you two will be *my* partners."

Mr. Mubashir put one hand on Nick's shoulder and one on Dinah's, as if they were preschoolers with their name tags pinned to the backs of their T-shirts.

"We are going outside for lunch now," he said. Flanked by Dinah and Nick, he led the group out the museum doors, down the steps, and across the street to the well-trampled lawn stretching before them. "We will have ourselves a nice picnic."

"Dinah ran away!" It was Artie again, behind her in line, taunting her. "It's too bad you weigh three hundred pounds. I guess all that weight slowed you down a bit, huh, Dinah?"

"Oh, shut up, Adams," Nick said. Artie shut up.

Nick leaned forward across Mr. Mubashir and gave Dinah a tentative smile. In that instant, Dinah forgave him for teasing her. She forgave him for his remarks to her after the debate. She even forgave him for winning the election. Nick's telling Artie to shut up was like Lancelot's defeating a hostile knight in a jousting tournament to defend Guinevere's honor. Not that the story of Lancelot and Guinevere had a particularly happy ending. Still, it was undeniably one of the great love stories of all time.

Dinah beamed a smile back at Nick, a smile shining as brightly as the Dinah Seabrooke star.

Eleven

"How was the trip to the museum?" Dinah's mother asked her when she got home that night, after having dinner at Suzanne's house. Benjamin was in bed, and both of her parents were sitting at the kitchen table, eating bowls of strawberry ice cream.

"Fine," Dinah said. The full story was too complicated to share.

"Fine?" her father asked, raising an eyebrow.

"Fine," Dinah repeated. Well, maybe she could tell them a bit more. "Nick and I made up. And I kind of got separated from my class for a while, and so did Nick, and they broadcast both of our names over the PA system for the whole entire museum to hear. And I need to earn twenty-five dollars so that I can have a star named after me. And Artie Adams threw up on the bus ride home. How was your biology exam?"

"Separated?" Dinah's mother asked, before her father could answer. "How did you get separated from your class?"

"It just sort of happened. Well, actually—you really want to hear the whole thing?"

"Please," Dinah's father said.

Dinah fixed herself a bowl of ice cream and settled down at the kitchen table. Then she launched into the full story. "So can I baby-sit for Benjamin sometime? To earn the money for my star?" she asked when she was done.

"Oh, Dinah," her mother said. Dinah always tried to make her stories as funny as possible, but her mother tended to sigh afterward, as if Dinah's stories were excruciatingly sad.

"I think we might have said yes *before* we heard this particular story," her father said. "But now I think— well, we're still not ready to try this again."

"Suzanne baby-sits all the time. So does Blaine."

"Did Suzanne and Blaine get separated from their class today?" her father asked.

"No, but—"

"All right, then," he said, as if he had proved his point.

"Then how am I going to earn twenty-five dollars?" Sometimes Dinah's parents made her so angry that it was all she could do not to hurl herself shrieking on the floor, like Benjamin.

"Well," Dinah's mother said. "Guess who called today?"

100

Dinah tried to remember if she was in trouble with any of her other teachers.

"Ruth Briscoe. She noticed the newspaper piles, too, when she was visiting her mother the other day, and she asked if I'd spend a few hours over there, helping her get reorganized—sort of a booster session. Do you want to be my assistant?"

"Yes!" Dinah said. Sometimes she loved her parents so much she had to hug them.

Then she remembered her first question again. "How *was* your exam?"

Her father grinned. "Our prof had the answers posted by the door when we left. I'm not sure what her curve will be like, but it looks like the worst I can get is a B."

Dinah gave her father a second hug. "I bet you got an A. If I were the teacher, I'd give you an A plus."

"It sure feels like an A plus to me," her father said.

Dinah sat back down at the table and scooped up her last melting spoonful of strawberry ice cream. Her father deserved an A plus. Dinah had never seen anyone work as hard as he had, even when he had been so discouraged after that first disappointing exam. It had been a long time since Dinah had seen him without his biology textbook. Even now it sat in front of him on the kitchen table, next to his empty ice-cream bowl. Once again Dinah marveled: How could someone who had only one life to live, in a solar system that was fast burning out, spend it studying biology? But her father certainly looked happy tonight as he picked up his empty ice-cream bowl and carried it to the sink.

Nick came over to Dinah's house on Saturday evening, with Suzanne and Greg, and the four of them lay on the floor in the family room, eating microwave popcorn and watching ancient episodes of a funny 1960s spy show that Nick had taped at home from late-night TV.

The shows were extremely silly, but Dinah found herself laughing anyway, leaning up against the family room's overstuffed couch, with Nick's arm around her. With his free hand, Nick fed Dinah buttery popcorn from his bowl, kernel by kernel. Nothing in Dinah's entire life had ever tasted so good. She held each kernel in her mouth as long as she could, until it finally dissolved into nothingness. Then she opened her mouth for another one.

Dinah wished that this moment could last, wouldn't fleet away like all the others. She wished she could put all her favorite moments in some special, magic box: this one, and moments at Mrs. Briscoe's house sipping tea, and some of the moments she had spent writing her poems. Those were almost the best moments: the moments after she had an idea for a poem, and then reached for a scrap of paper and a well-chewed pen, and began writing, lost to everything else in the world except the scratching of her pen on the paper and the words that were trying to form themselves into verses on the page.

Dinah felt an urge for a poem right now. She didn't want to pull away from Nick's embrace to find a piece of paper, so she closed her eyes and tuned out the television and tried shaping the lines in her mind.

> I wish tonight
> Could always be—
> Me with you,
> And you with me.
>
> But if this night must fade away
> And with it everything that's in it,
> Could I make one small request
> And keep forever just this minute?

At Mrs. Briscoe's house on Sunday afternoon, Dinah helped her mother reorganize Mrs. Briscoe's kitchen pantry shelves—the same shelves that she had helped organize a year before.

"This is how you get clutter," her mother told Dinah in a low voice. "Five boxes of macaroni, all opened, all three-quarters empty. The solution: a canister, of course. Here, this empty mayonnaise jar will do for now."

Dinah poured the macaroni into the jar.

"Or over here. Twelve cans of stewed tomatoes, obviously bought on sale. It's sensible to stock up on a bargain item, but the overflow cans should be moved to the top shelf, out of the way. They shouldn't be blocking everything else."

Dinah handed the extra cans, two by two, to her mother.

"I think the pantry's pretty well under control now," Dinah's mother said. "Why don't you go keep Mrs. Briscoe company for a while? I know she gets nervous when we're in here rummaging about."

Dinah found Mrs. Briscoe on the front porch. Mrs. Briscoe loved to sit on her front porch, looking out over the late-blooming wildflowers in her front yard, watching the birds that came flocking to her feeder.

"I wanted to stay out of your mother's way," Mrs. Briscoe said. "Is she very disappointed in me for letting all her good work from last year come undone?"

"Oh, no," Dinah said honestly. "She likes organizing people. She doesn't mind doing it over and over again. She even told me so once."

Dinah sat quietly for a minute, watching a plump squirrel feasting on the sunflower seeds that lay thick on the ground beneath the bird feeder. Then she said, "Do you ever think it's strange, how people meet? Like how you and I met? If I hadn't been helping my mother last year, we never would have met. Or if Nick's father hadn't been transferred to Riverdale, Nick and I wouldn't have met."

When Dinah had met Mrs. Briscoe for the first time a year before, she had never dreamed that the birdlike woman with the astonishingly messy house would become one of her closest friends, any more than she had dreamed that the obnoxious boy teasing her all the time at school would become her boyfriend. Life certainly took many strange twists and turns.

"It's amazing," Mrs. Briscoe agreed.

"How did you and Mr. Briscoe meet? The very first time?"

"Well, we lived in a small town, where everybody knew everybody else, so we would have been hard-pressed not to meet. If we hadn't met in one way, we would have met in another."

"But how *did* you meet?"

"Eddie was driving a delivery truck for the local grocery store. One day my doorbell rang, and there was this handsome young man trying to deliver an order of pork chops to my folks. I kept trying to explain to him that we hadn't ordered any pork chops, and he kept insisting that his order was plainly marked with our address. By the time we got it all straightened out, we had pretty much figured out that we enjoyed each other's company."

"Was it love at first sight?" Dinah asked. "For me and Nick, it was more like hate at first sight."

"Love?" Mrs. Briscoe asked. "Love takes a long time. But I was interested, I have to admit it."

"So if there hadn't been a mixup over pork chops, you might have married someone else," Dinah said.

"Well, as I said, in a small town, there aren't too many surprises. But there are some. Maybe Eddie was mine."

Nick had definitely been a surprise to Dinah. But in a way, everything in life was a surprise. Just about every day something happened that Dinah hadn't expected, like a poem, or a kiss from Nick, or a chance to buy her very own star.

"Did you know that for twenty-five dollars you can have a star named after you?" Dinah asked. "I've earned the money for mine today, helping my mother. I'm sending away for it tonight. Do you want to get one, too? Suzanne doesn't. She says she'll just look at mine."

"I'll look at yours, too," Mrs. Briscoe said. "What a lovely idea, naming a star. And there's no one I'd rather see a star named for than you."

Above the trees across from Mrs. Briscoe's house, the evening star appeared in the darkening sky. Dinah knew it was not really a star but the planet Venus.

"There's Venus," Mrs. Briscoe said, as if reading Dinah's thoughts.

Another moment for Dinah to save.

"I wrote a new poem last night," Dinah said. She recited it softly for Mrs. Briscoe. Last night, as she had been writing it, it had been for Nick, but now it was for Mrs. Briscoe, too.

When Dinah finished, Mrs. Briscoe reached over and took her hand. The two of them sat together on the porch swing without speaking, side by side, hand in hand, until Dinah's mother came outside for Dinah, and it was time to go home.

Twelve

Ms. Dunne usually wore suits. On Monday her suit was a brilliant lime green. She looked to Dinah like a lime Popsicle. Her two legs were the Popsicle sticks.

"I am very proud of the poetry you have all been writing for me this fall," Ms. Dunne told the class at the start of second period. "I always expect great things from my seventh graders, but this time my expectations have already been far exceeded. In fact, I think it's time your poetry was shared with a wider audience."

That was exactly what Dinah had expected Ms. Dunne to say to her the other day. At least Ms. Dunne was saying it now, even if she *was* speaking to the whole class.

"Mr. Roemer has agreed to let us have the large bulletin board in front of the main office," Ms. Dunne continued. "Every week from now on, from one of my four seventh-grade classes, I'm going to choose a Poet of the Week. That person's poems will be prominently displayed on the front bulletin board for all to see. So over the course of the year, some thirty of you will have your work featured in this way. As I have over a hundred seventh-grade students, this will be a significant honor. And at the end of year, we'll gather all the Poet of the Week poems into a book that we'll donate to our school library."

"Who's going to be the first Poet of the Week?" someone asked.

Dinah waited for the reply. She would have asked the question herself, but it seemed impolite for the most obvious choice for Poet of the Week to call attention to herself in that way. She looked down modestly at her desk, in case everyone was staring at her.

"I haven't decided yet," Ms. Dunne said. "Really, the talent in my classes this year is overwhelming. I'll make my decision as soon as possible."

Dinah herself hadn't noticed any other overwhelming talent in the second-period class, but perhaps there were some outstanding poets in Ms. Dunne's other classes. The thought was a sobering one.

"I want to have the first Poet of the Week on display next Monday," Ms. Dunne went on. "Does anyone have any new poems to hand in today?"

Dinah opened her notebook. She wasn't going to hand in the poem she'd written on Saturday night, even though she thought it was the best poem she'd ever written. It was too close to her heart to share with anyone except Nick and Mrs. Briscoe. Instead she took out her latest collection of haiku and read them over one last time:

The clouds hide the sun.
Crickets chirp in the evening
As winter draws near.

A dead bird lay still
On the sidewalk this morning,
His song now silent.

Today is over.
It is finished forever,
Never to return.

They were still about death, but they weren't as *much* about death as "A Few Thoughts on Immigration Policy." They were just right, Dinah thought, for the Poet of the Week.

The second practice debate was held after school on Wednesday. Dinah and Nick debated two eighth graders, this time arguing *for* stronger regulations on immigration. Dinah made her speeches as dull as she possibly could. No one could accuse her this time of being emotional or dramatic. Well-chosen statistics? Dinah didn't know how well chosen her statistics were, but she certainly had a tall stack of three-by-five file cards covered with them, though the stack would have been taller if she and her partner hadn't spent a full week refusing to speak to each other.

Dinah and Nick lost again.

"I said you shouldn't try to get by on emotion," Mr. Dixon said afterward. "I didn't say you should be *dead*."

"I hope you're happy," Dinah told Nick as they walked to the bus together. "I toned down the dramatics and look what happened."

"*Tone down* doesn't mean *eliminate completely*," Nick said. "It just means *tone down*. Come on, let's not fight. Next time we can just tone *up* the dramatics. Like maybe halfway up."

Dinah knew she couldn't blame Nick for their defeat, though it was tempting to try. "Okay," she said. "Next time we'll be right in the middle."

Next time she and Nick would work harder, too, for now they were back together again, back together to stay.

Ms. Dunne didn't announce the first Poet of the Week until Thursday morning.

"I'm pleased to say that the first Poet of the Week will be from our second-period class," Ms. Dunne said, once the bell had sounded and everyone was seated.

Dinah hardly breathed. Poet of the Week wasn't the same as Poet of All Eternity, but it was better than nothing—than being snuffed out of life with no fame whatsoever. Maybe at the end of the year the Poet of the Week book could be published by a real publisher, so that it would be in libraries all over America, and in the big Library of Congress in Washington, D.C. Dinah would suggest it.

If she won.

But she had to win. How could she *not* win?

"Our first Poet of the Week is distinguished by both the quantity and the quality of her work."

Her work. And Dinah knew she wrote more poems than anyone else in her class. And they *were* the best, they were. That was just a fact, the way it was a fact that the sun was 93 million miles away from the earth.

"Our poet writes in a wide range of styles: rhyming verse, free verse, haiku. And her poetry treats serious and important themes in a thoughtful and striking way. Our first Poet of the Week is Dinah Seabrooke."

The class applauded. Dinah bent her head graciously to acknowledge their cheers. Well, maybe no one was actually cheering, but they were clapping pretty hard, especially Suzanne and Nick.

"Congratulations, Dinah," Ms. Dunne said. "Stop by for a few minutes after school today so we can select which of your poems to display. I'll take a picture of you, too, to mount on the bulletin board along with your poetry."

Dinah could hardly wait. Already her thoughts were racing. Maybe Mr. Roemer would read "A Few Thoughts on Immigration Policy" over morning announcements, as he had read Longfellow's "Psalm of

Life." Maybe she could arrange to have it broadcast over the PA system in the Air and Space Museum. . . .

When Dinah walked into JFK Middle School on Monday morning, the first thing she saw was the bulletin board for Poet of the Week. There was her picture—gazing poetically off into the distance—and a dozen of her poems, including "In a Mere Five Billion Years," "A Few Thoughts on Immigration Policy," and the best of her haiku.

All day long, Dinah collected compliments, or at least comments. Mr. Dixon wasn't one for compliments, but he stopped her in the hall to say, "Saw your poem on immigration. Now, don't start spouting poetry on us in the next debate, Seabrooke." Miss Brady, Dinah's gym teacher, who had never seemed in the least poetic, asked Dinah for a copy of one of her haiku. Mr. Mubashir read her poem about the sun out loud to the entire eighth-period science class.

Mr. Roemer didn't read any of Dinah's poems over morning announcements, but he did announce her name as Poet of the Week and told all the students of JFK Middle School to be sure to admire her work on the front bulletin board.

Maybe it was the poetic aura that clung to Dinah like a gauzy veil, maybe it was the hard work she and Nick had put in all weekend, but Dinah and Nick won their next practice debate, and against the other two eighth graders, too.

"This time you had it all," Mr. Dixon told them.

112

"Substance *and* style. Even if we're all going to die in the end, eh, Seabrooke?"

It was definitely Dinah's favorite week of seventh grade so far. She wouldn't at all mind leaving her footprints on the sands of time as a famous poet and debater. And more good things lay ahead: Mr. Mubashir had announced that this coming Friday evening, their class would gather for its first stargazing. They would meet on the school lawn at nine o'clock to learn how to recognize fall constellations. And maybe somewhere out there in the star-spangled heavens would be Dinah's own star. She should be hearing back from the star registry any day now, informing her which star would be the one to be named after JFK Middle School's first-ever Poet of the Week.

On Thursday morning, Ms. Dunne smiled at the class. "Dinah's week as our official seventh-grade poet is almost over. I've now chosen the second Poet of the Week. Next week I really am going to select a poet from one of my other classes. I don't want anyone to think that I favor second period. But the poet I've chosen has improved so much over the past few weeks that I simply have to recognize him next."

Dinah felt a pang of sadness. She didn't want her week to be over. She didn't want to come to school next week and see someone else's poems on the bulletin board. Suddenly Dinah couldn't bear the fleetingness of fame. Five billion years had seemed short enough. A week was nothing.

"Our second Poet of the Week, by contrast with our

first poet, writes comic poetry. He has a keen sense of humor, which he is learning to express in successful rhyming verse."

Dinah glanced over at Nick. He was very funny, though most of the poems he had shown her this fall had been serious. If someone else had to be Poet of the Week, Dinah hoped it was Nick.

"Our second Poet of the Week," Ms. Dunne said with a twinkle in her eye, "is Artie Adams."

Dinah stared at Artie in horror. If this was a joke, it wasn't funny. She expected Artie to gag and retch, to give a good imitation of himself throwing up on Mr. Mubashir's class trip. But instead Artie looked pleased and almost shy. The others clapped, even louder for Artie than they had for Dinah. This time they definitely *were* cheering.

Poet of the Week! Joke of the Week! The sooner Dinah's week ended, the better.

At the end of class, Dinah still felt as cruelly betrayed as she had at the beginning. She stood motionless by her desk, waiting for Suzanne and Nick to come to her, to denounce Ms. Dunne's monstrously inappropriate choice.

Suzanne knew what to say. "Artie?" she whispered to Dinah. "It's easy to be most improved if you start at negative a billion."

But Nick stopped by Artie's desk and gave him a high five. Dinah wouldn't have believed it if she hadn't seen it with her own eyes. This was hardly Lancelot jousting in a tournament to defend the honor of Guinevere.

Then he came over to Dinah and tried to take her hand. Dinah snatched it away and held it clenched in a tight fist behind her back.

"Hey, what's with you?" Nick asked. "You're not —you can't be all bent out of shape just because of Artie."

"Yes, I can," Dinah said.

"But, look, Dunne said there are going to be thirty kids picked for this thing. She's bound to pick someone or other you're not wild about. I know Artie's a loud-mouth, but you have to admit he *is* funny."

"I do not."

"*Someone* had to be the next Poet of the Week." Nick followed Dinah out into the hall. "And it's not like—I mean, let's face it, Poet of the Week in one dumb class at one dumb school is not that big a deal."

Dinah felt as if she had been slapped. How could something so important to her mean so little to Nick? Dinah knew then, as certainly as she knew anything in the world, that she and Nick were over, through, fin-ished, kaput, separated by a chasm too large to be bridged anytime in the next five billion years.

"I admit it's not like being class *president*," Dinah snapped. "It may not be a big deal to you, but it hap-pens to be a big deal to me. I'm going to *die* someday, and my poems are all I have that's going to live after me."

115

"We're *all* going to die," Nick said. "You act like you're the only one."

"I do not." The author of "A Few Thoughts on Immigration Policy" plainly recognized that everyone was going to die. And yet . . . deep down, Dinah knew that Nick was right. Other people could die, and the world would go on, for another few billion years or so, but how could it go on with no more Dinah Seabrooke? How could it go on without *her*? Maybe, all along, Dinah hadn't minded so much that the sun would burn out someday as that the sun would keep shining, temporarily at least, even when there was no more Dinah for it to shine upon.

"You know what?" Nick said, as if he were reading Dinah's thoughts. "The world can get along just fine without you, and me, and Artie—without all of us. Look at it this way. It got along without us for a few billion years before we were born."

Dinah felt her old anger flaring, the rage that burned hot inside her like the thermonuclear reactions at the interior of the sun. If she wasn't going to have even one pathetic shred of immortality, nothing in life was worth striving for or struggling to hold on to—certainly not a relationship with someone who could hurt her as badly as Nick had today.

"I'm sure *you* can get along just fine without me, starting now," Dinah said. "And I'll get along just fine without you."

The bell rang. Nick turned to go to his next class. Dinah stood alone in the deserted corridor, in front of her Poet of the Week bulletin board. She reached up and took down her picture and ripped it in two, the way she should have torn up Nick's postcards all those weeks ago, the cards that still lay buried in her bureau drawer. Then she walked away, leaving both love and fame behind her.

Thirteen

Somehow Dinah got through the rest of her classes and the after-school rehearsal for *Carousel*. She wanted the day to be over, and the week to be over, and the year to be over. Dinah didn't think she could stand it if the rest of seventh grade—if the rest of her life—was like this. How did other people get through life, when there was nothing, nothing at all, worth living for?

Once Mrs. Bevens finally dismissed the cast, Dinah hurried outside, on her way to Mrs. Briscoe's house. She needed to tell Mrs. Briscoe about this final fight with Nick; she had to hear Mrs. Briscoe say that *she* understood why Dinah had felt so hurt when Nick had sneered at her one small seventh-grade triumph. Mrs. Briscoe would say that Dinah had been right to break up with Nick one last, final time. Dinah needed a cup of hot tea poured from a frog teapot to soothe the stubborn lump of unshed tears crowding her throat.

"Dinah."

Dinah whirled around. Her mother was walking toward her from her parked car.

"I was hoping I'd catch you before you left," her mother said.

Dinah looked at her, puzzled. Her mother had never stopped by school before. The afternoon had turned chilly, but her mother wasn't wearing a coat.

"Dinah, honey, I have some bad news. Ruth Briscoe just called. Mrs. Briscoe had a heart attack this morning, and—oh, honey, she's gone."

Dinah didn't understand. "Gone?"

"She was drinking a cup of tea on her front porch. One of the neighbors found her. The doctor says she probably died instantly."

Dinah still didn't understand. It didn't make sense.

"But I was just going over there, to see her."

"I was afraid you might be. That's why as soon as I heard, I got in the car to look for you. Dinah, I'm so sorry."

"But . . ."

Dinah didn't know what to say. Mrs. Briscoe couldn't be—*dead*. She didn't even know that Dinah was Poet of the Week. Dinah had meant to go over to Mrs. Briscoe's house last weekend, but she and Nick had been working on the debate. And then this week she'd been so busy, with rehearsals and everything. So Mrs. Briscoe didn't know that Dinah and Nick had finally won a debate. Or that Poet of the Week had turned out to be a big joke. Or that Dinah and Nick had just broken up again, this time forever. Mrs. Briscoe couldn't be *dead*.

"But I didn't get to— There's a bunch of things I didn't get to tell her—and I didn't get to say good-bye or anything."

"I know, honey. This is very sudden."

Dinah's mother put her arm around her and led her to the car. Dinah thought: I should be crying. But she wasn't crying. It didn't seem real. It seemed more like a mistake, or a dream, or a scene from a play. Dinah could almost see the lines printed out, as in the script for *Carousel*:

MOTHER: Oh, Dinah, I'm sorry. Mrs. Briscoe is dead.
DINAH: But she can't be dead.
MOTHER: It happened this morning, while she was
    sitting out on her front porch.
DINAH: But she can't be *dead*.

They seemed like lines Dinah had memorized and practiced with Suzanne. In the play, there would be a stage direction, for the actress playing Dinah to cry. But Dinah didn't think she could cry, except in fake, stagy sobs. She didn't feel sad. She didn't feel anything at all.

Dinah was silent on the ride home. Her mother didn't say anything, either. She just reached across to Dinah at traffic lights and held her hand. They passed the after-school-activities bus, with Suzanne on it. They passed children playing in the park. Nobody looked any different. It was just an ordinary afternoon, except that Mrs. Briscoe was dead.

When they got home, Dinah's mother sat down on the family room couch and pulled Dinah down onto her lap. It had been a long time since her mother had held her like that. These days her lap was usually filled with Benjamin. The unexpected cuddle added to the strangeness, making Dinah feel even more as if she were trapped inside the script for a play.

MOTHER (*holding Dinah on her lap*): I called your father at the store. He's going to come home early.

DINAH: That's good.

MOTHER: I have to get Benjamin in a few minutes. Do you want to come?

DINAH: Okay.

MOTHER: Ruth Briscoe said the funeral will be on Saturday, at two o'clock.

DINAH: Oh.

Dinah had never been to a funeral before. She had never known someone who'd died.

She walked with her mother to get Benjamin from day care at Mrs. Haywood's, three blocks away. Her mother didn't tell Benjamin about Mrs. Briscoe. He was too little to understand.

At home again, Dinah didn't know what to do. What are you supposed to do on the day one of your best friends dies?

"Why don't you call Suzanne?" her mother suggested. "She was fond of Mrs. Briscoe. And Nick will want to know, too."

Dinah didn't bother telling her mother that she and Nick had broken up again, this time for good. Mechanically, she dialed Suzanne's number. Mrs. Kelly answered the phone.

"Suzanne's downstairs practicing the piano. I'll get her," Mrs. Kelly said. "Is something wrong, Dinah?"

"Yes," Dinah said. "My friend—our friend—Mrs. Briscoe? She died."

"Oh, Dinah, I'm so sorry. Suzanne! It's Dinah! Was it sudden?" Mrs. Kelly asked.

"She had a heart attack. This morning."

"How old was she?" Mrs. Kelly asked.

"Eighty-three."

"Well, she lived a long, full life, and it's a blessing that she went at the end without any suffering."

Dinah knew Mrs. Kelly was just trying to say something comforting. But she didn't feel comforted.

"Hello?" It was Suzanne, picking up the downstairs phone.

"I'll let you two talk now. Good-bye, Dinah. I'm so sorry."

"What happened?" Suzanne asked.

"It's Mrs. Briscoe. She had a heart attack. She died, this morning."

"Oh, Dinah!" On the other end of the phone, Dinah could hear Suzanne crying. The soft sound of Suzanne's weeping made Dinah feel even more numb inside. Suzanne was crying. Why wasn't she?

"I'd better go now," Dinah said. Not that she had anywhere to go. But she didn't know what else to say.

She felt like calling Nick, but he had never met Mrs. Briscoe. Dinah had told him a little bit about Mrs. Briscoe. But she had told Mrs. Briscoe so much about Nick that she felt that the two of them had known each other, even if the knowing had been almost entirely one-sided.

"Dinah!" her mother called her from the kitchen. "You got some mail. It's in here, on the kitchen table."

Dinah walked slowly into the kitchen. Was it wrong to look at mail when someone you loved had just died? Obviously her mother didn't think so. Still, guilt gnawed at Dinah.

The return address on the letter read International Star Registry. Dinah carefully tore open the envelope. Inside was an official document. Star number NGC 7822 had been registered in the name of Dinah Marie Seabrooke. The paper was embossed with a fancy-looking seal.

Dinah's very own star! She would put the letter on her bulletin board in her bedroom, right next to her bed. But first she had to show it to her parents, and Suzanne, and Mrs. Briscoe—

Mrs. Briscoe. She couldn't show it to Mrs. Briscoe.

The tears came then, in a blinding rush, and Dinah's mother held her in her arms and cried with her.

Fourteen

Ruth Briscoe called again that evening. Dinah's father kept his hand on her shoulder as Dinah took the receiver.

"Dinah. I've been going through some of my mother's papers, notes she left me about how she wanted things handled if— Well. We're having the funeral this Saturday, at two o'clock, at St. Paul's United Methodist Church. Mother picked out the songs she wanted and passages of Scripture, but she also asked if you would take part in the service. You write poetry? It's hard for me to make out her writing here, but I think she wanted you to read one of your poems. Dinah? Are you still there?"

"I'm here. I will. I want to."

"She also left you some money, five thousand dollars, for you to put aside for your education someday. You know she had no grandchildren; I'm her only child, and I never married. I think she thought of you as the granddaughter she never had. And she made a note that she wanted you to have her collection of frogs and toads, and her frog teapot."

Tears streamed down Dinah's face. Silently she handed her father the phone.

Friday morning, Dinah got up and got dressed and rode the bus to school with Suzanne. It felt bizarre to be going through the motions of an ordinary day. Yesterday Mrs. Briscoe had died during the morning, while Dinah had been at school, fuming about Poet of the Week. Mrs. Briscoe had been dead, but Dinah hadn't known it. Today Dinah knew, and that meant that nothing else in her life could ever be the same.

After reading the morning announcements, Mr. Roemer ended his broadcast by saying, "We have had an unfortunate incident this week in which some student took down one of the items on display on one of our school bulletin boards. I want to remind all of you that no one is to post any material on any bulletin board or remove any material from any bulletin board without authorization from the front office. The material on the bulletin boards is placed there for *everyone* to enjoy. Have a good day."

Dinah knew he was talking about her picture on the Poet of the Week bulletin board. In sixth grade, Dinah had thought that there was no greater thrill than to be the secret star of morning announcements, the unnamed individual singled out in one of Mr. Roemer's little "reminders."

Now she couldn't believe she had ever cared. She just wanted it to be yesterday morning, when Mrs. Briscoe was still alive and she and Nick were still together, rather than today, when she and Nick had broken up forever and Mrs. Briscoe was dead.

In math, Ms. Lewis handed back their midterm tests. In English, Ms. Dunne conducted their weekly grammar lesson. In gym class, Miss Brady took them outside for field hockey. It was a warm, clear day with a breathtakingly blue sky. But Mrs. Briscoe would never see the sky again.

Dinah ate lunch with Suzanne. "Did you tell Nick yet about Mrs. Briscoe?" Suzanne asked.

Dinah swallowed a mouthful of milk. "We broke up again yesterday. Remember?"

Actually, Dinah still found herself wanting to talk to Nick. It seemed odd that Nick, who had been her boyfriend up until the end of second period yesterday, didn't know that something so major and shattering had happened in her life. But that was what it meant to break up with someone: that your life and his life were no longer intertwined.

"You haven't made up yet?" Suzanne asked.

"*No*. This time it really *is* over. It really is *over* over."

"It's not over," Suzanne said. "You and Nick aren't over. I know you, and I know Nick. You'll be back together again tomorrow."

Dinah shook her head. "This is different. Sometimes

things really *are* over. It's like—Mrs. Briscoe really is dead. And you and I—we're really going to die, too. And the sun is really going to burn out. I forgot to tell you, my star came yesterday, my Dinah star. But it doesn't really change anything."

"Do you think you'll see it? When we go out stargazing with Mr. Mubashir tonight? Would you know which one it is?"

"No. I mean, it'll look just like a *star*. And there are a hundred billion stars just in *our* galaxy, plus all the stars in everybody else's galaxies."

A hundred billion galaxies, each with a hundred billion stars. It made Dinah feel amazingly *small*.

After school, Dinah tried to work on her poem for Mrs. Briscoe. Nothing came. She had been writing poems about death for weeks, but now that someone she loved had really truly died, she didn't know what to say. And the funeral was less than twenty-four hours away.

Dinah's father, home early from the store, looked up from his biology book. "Stuck? What about reading one of your other poems? You have so many. One of them would probably be all right."

"They're not. They're all so—depressing. It's like, people are already going to be depressed at a funeral. I don't want to make them feel even worse. But death *is* depressing. It just is."

Even Dinah's beautiful poem about saving moments seemed depressing now, because the terrible truth was that there was no special, magic box in which moments could be saved. Every moment of Mrs. Briscoe's life had evaporated into nothingness.

Dinah's father closed his book. "Why don't you write a poem about life, then?" he asked. "Life isn't depressing."

"But it *is*. When everybody's just going to *die* in the end, it is."

"Mrs. Briscoe didn't think so," Dinah's father said gently. "She knew that she was going to die someday, and some day not so terribly far away, and I got the impression that she still thought life was pretty wonderful."

That was true. Dinah had never known Mrs. Briscoe to be depressed. She had been interested in flowers, birds, frogs, poetry, immigration policy, and Dinah. At eighty-three, close to death, she had been one of the most alive people Dinah had ever known. Never once had Mrs. Briscoe given up on living.

"I don't know if I can write a poem about life," Dinah said. "When I was Poet of the Week, the whole bulletin board was poems on death."

"You can try," her father said. "That's all we can ever do, is try."

Dinah picked up her pen and stared down at her blank sheet of paper. For Mrs. Briscoe, she would try. Mrs. Briscoe's frog teapot had been her last gift to Dinah. The poem would be Dinah's last gift to Mrs. Briscoe.

———

When Suzanne's mother dropped Suzanne and Dinah off at school that evening, the sky was moonless and cloudless, a perfect night for stargazing. Mr. Mubashir greeted them in the parking lot, looking jaunty in his heavy jacket with a long hand-knit scarf streaming down behind him. In the darkness, Dinah reached for Suzanne's hand. It was magical to be out at night looking at stars together.

Nick was there, joking around on the other side of the group with Artie. He looked very handsome, in a rugged outdoorsy jacket that Dinah had never seen before. Everything seemed so different at night that Dinah almost felt like going up to Nick and trying to make up with him one last time. But how many times can you break up with somebody forever and then get back together again?

"All right, class," Mr. Mubashir said. "I think everyone is here. Let's begin our tour of the October sky. There, above the trees?" Mr. Mubashir pointed. "That is the most familiar of all constellations, the Big Dipper, part of the constellation called Ursa Major, the Great Bear."

The Big Dipper was one of the few constellations Dinah could already recognize. It was hard to believe that even the stars of the Big Dipper would someday die, would proceed through their life cycle and become red giants and then white dwarfs, and then—nothing: just empty space where once a star had shone.

Mr. Mubashir showed them how to use the Pointers

in the Big Dipper to find Polaris, the North Star. Even *Polaris* would burn out one day.

Overhead Dinah could see hundreds, probably thousands, of stars shining brightly, despite the competition from the nighttime lights of Riverdale. But the stars Dinah could see with her naked eye were only the smallest fraction of a hundred billion stars multiplied by a hundred billion galaxies. Mr. Mubashir had written the number on the board in class one day: 100 followed by 20 zeroes. If you tried to count all the stars in the universe, at a rate of one per second, you wouldn't finish for 316 *trillion* years.

The hugeness of the universe pressed down on Dinah. Somewhere in that vastness shone Star NGC 7822. And somewhere in that vastness was Mrs. Briscoe. She had to be somewhere: She couldn't just be *gone*.

Mr. Mubashir handed out sheets of paper on which two semicircles were printed, representing the northern and southern hemispheres of the sky. Using the flashlights they had brought from home, they were supposed to face north and try to draw every star they saw, then do the same thing facing south.

Dinah faced north. It was hard to pick out any constellations other than the two Dippers and Cassiopeia. The stars didn't jump out at her in patterns; they just twinkled in a jumble of pulsing light.

"Dinah."

Nick was there behind her. "Suzanne told me about your friend, Mrs. Briscoe. I just wanted to say—well, that I'm sorry. I know how close the two of you were. It has to be rough—losing a friend like that."

Dinah didn't feel herself reaching out for Nick's hand, but suddenly she was holding on to it, so tightly that Nick's fingers must have hurt.

"It's awful," she said. "It's like—do you believe in heaven? Do you think people go to heaven when they die?"

"I guess so," Nick said. "I mean, the person's body gets buried or cremated or something, but the *person* still has to be somewhere."

Dinah looked down. She was still holding Nick's hand. Did that mean that they had unbroken up again? What did she want it to mean?

"I'm sorry," Dinah said then, slowly. "About yesterday. Getting so mad about Poet of the Week. I don't know why I get so mad at you all the time. It's like—I just get so *mad*."

"Mount St. Dinah," Nick said. "You know, like Mount St. Helens. The volcano? But, yeah, it's pretty horrible when you erupt. Then again, it's pretty nice in between eruptions."

Nick drew Dinah close to him. Dinah knew he was going to kiss her. She wanted him to, and yet—

Love was so *hard*. Dinah didn't know how anybody managed to do it, to make it last. Of course, for most people it didn't last. Dinah knew one girl at school who had already had three different boyfriends just in seventh grade. Blaine Yarborough's parents were divorced, and so were Jason Winfield's. Even Mrs. Briscoe had once been so angry at Mr. Briscoe that she had locked him outside on the front stoop.

But love was wonderful, too. There was nothing else

in the universe like it. Catching fireflies with Nick, sharing popcorn, debating, laughing, kissing—all of it had been worth living for, every minute of it. Even if no single moment could be saved for all of time, that was no reason not to savor every moment as fully as you could while you were lucky enough to be living it. Neither love nor life would last forever, but both were still full of astonishing and joyful surprises.

Nick kissed Dinah. His kiss might not have gone on for all eternity, but it seemed as if it did.

"Here," Nick said, "I made this for you ten minutes ago, when I was supposed to be drawing stars."

He handed Dinah a folded piece of paper. She opened it, and by the light of her flashlight she saw that Nick had drawn a piece of cream pie. And on the piece of pie he had written her name.

Dinah drew as many stars on her chart as she could, but there were so many stars that finally she gave up and just made random dots all over the page with the tip of her pencil.

Then she sat down with her back against the trunk of a bare tree. She turned the chart over, and on the back, leaning it against her knees, by the light of her flashlight, she began scribbling her poem for Mrs. Briscoe.

> I look up at the starry sky
> With stars as far as I can see.

Mrs. Briscoe is there somewhere.
I wish that she were here with me.

People die, but love lives on.
Love is what will always be.
It will always be a fact
That I loved her, and she loved me.

Beneath the sky, the earth is dark,
Yet stars twinkle up above.
They will die, and I will die,
But what lives on is love.

Dinah was crying again when she put her pencil down. She still wasn't sure the poem said what she wanted it to say. It wasn't really true that love lived on—in the end, nothing would live on—but in the meantime, in the short run, in the here and now, love was one reason to keep on living. Poetry was another.

Suddenly Dinah knew that it didn't matter, really, that no one would read her poems in another five billion years, once the sun had burned out. The purpose of writing poetry wasn't to be named Poet of the Week or Poet of All Eternity; the purpose of writing poetry was just—to write poetry. Dinah wrote poetry because nothing else made her feel more fully and truly alive.

"Is everyone finished?" Mr. Mubashir called. "Bring me your star charts as soon as you are done."

Dinah couldn't turn in her star chart, because she had written her poem for Mrs. Briscoe on the back of it. She had a feeling that Mr. Mubashir would understand. Carefully she folded her poem and tucked it into her jacket pocket, next to Nick's drawing. Then, shivering with cold and happiness, she waited for Suzanne beneath the night's vast, endless canopy of glittering stars.